ZOMBIES

ZOMBIES

The Complete Guide to the World of the Living Dead

Zachary Graves

CHARTWELL
BOOKS, INC.

CONTENTS

CONTENTS

INTRODUCTION

The age of the zombie has arrived. In recent years, the zombie has joined vampires, werewolves, and ghouls as a popular addition to the horror pantheon, becoming a familiar figure on screen (whether in film, TV, or computer games), in fiction, and even in pop and rock music. With movies like *Night of the Living Dead* and its various sequels and remakes, video games such as the *Resident Evil* series (which has sold a staggering 40 million copies worldwide) and the current spate of post-modern 'mash-up' novels like *Pride and Prejudice and Zombies*, the zombie is beginning to establish itself as one of our favourite denizens of the world of the undead. Indeed, zombie has even begun to outstrip vampires in popularity, with zombie films and fiction providing the same kind of smart, up-to-date entertainment for young males that the *Twilight* phenomenon offers to adolescent girls.

At first glance, it may be hard to understand the zombie's appeal. The zombie has none of the dark, sexy glamour of its undead cousin the vampire; and it entirely lacks the mystery, nobility and beauty – albeit vicious and violent – of that other infamous medieval revenant, the werewolf. The zombie, in its most common manifestation, is a slow, stupid, shuffling creature, with vacant eyes and a grey, expressionless face. It is hideously ugly, a rotting corpse from the grave, covered in blood and gore, and emitting a sickening stench. Parts of its body may be missing; it may have severed limbs, open wounds, or entrails hanging out from its insides. Far from being sexy or attractive in any way, it is the most disgusting, repulsive creature imaginable. Yet, as far as Western popular culture goes, it is clear that we can't get enough of the zombie. We love them. Why?

HORROR AND COMEDY

The answer is that the zombie myth explores some of the most disturbing aspects of modern life, from the serious to the mundane, from the horrific to the comical. The vampire may have evolved, in literature, from a medieval monster much like the zombie – a gruesome revenant from the grave, dripping with blood and gore – into the suave, refined ladies' man that we know today, but the zombie has resolutely refused to follow this path. It remains revolting, uncivilised, and vile. We are horrified by its disgusting appearance and repulsive body, but also sometimes amused by the sheer grossness of its antics, whether pulling off a victim's arm and snacking on it, or slicing the top off someone's head and supping on warm human brains. This mixture of horror and comedy is the essence of the zombie's appeal to adolescent boys – and that means the adolescent boy in all of us. The zombie is funny, in the way that cartoons are funny, because it takes our darkest fears about the vulnerability of our human body and makes a comedy of them, relieving us of our fear of being harmed, and our dread of death, if only for the duration of watching a film, playing a game, or reading a book.

But there is more to the zombie, and the phenomenon of its popularity today, than sheer entertainment value. As well as making us laugh, and delivering the usual thrills and shocks of the horror genre, the zombie narrative also helps us to explore some of the most pressing issues in modern society, sometimes light-heartedly, sometimes more seriously. There are plenty of zombie movies, games and novels that merely pile on the gore, but to become a classic in the genre, the work must also offer a witty, insightful and perhaps ironic commentary on the contradictions and difficulties of modern life. This is no mean feat: slathering on zombie

gore, delivering bucketloads of blood, and, at the same time, presenting an intelligent, thoughtful critique of contemporary civilisation and its ills is not an easy task. However, it has been done, to a greater or lesser extent, in classic films such as George Romero's *Night of the Living Dead* and its sequels, which take their visual cue from the slick DC comics of the fifties such as *Tales from the Crypt*, mixing cartoon style violence with a radical reappraisal of the values and morals of American culture.

Romero's approach, itself inspired by apocalyptic science fiction of the 1950s, such as Richard Matheson's *I Am Legend*, has continued to set the pattern of the modern zombie horror movie: dumb, tasteless 'B' movie violence, clever visual gags and, underlying the entire presentation of the narrative, a deeply critical, often pessimistic view of human nature and civilisation.

EXPLOITATION OF THE MASSES

The themes explored in the zombie legend are many: the exploitation of the masses in capitalist society, the soullessness of modern-day life, our fear of a global apocalypse, our revulsion at the reality of war, and the inevitability of death, to name the most salient of them. If we look at each of these issues in turn, we may begin to understand why the figure of the zombie has begun to play such an important part in popular culture today.

The legend of the zombie arose in West Africa, where it formed part of the religion known as Vodun, and centred around a deity or *loa* known as the Grand Zombi, a snake god. It was brought by African slaves to the island of Haiti, where it became incorporated into the folklore of the people. This was a mixture of African spiritual beliefs and Catholic teachings, so that the African *loa,* or spirit gods, became interchangeable with the Catholic saints, in a religion that came to be known as Vodou, or Voodoo. In this religion, a zombie came to mean a person whose soul had been captured by a sorceror or *bokor*, and who was forced to live out a miserable existence as the *bokor's* slave.

Early zombie tales tell of *bokors* using zombies to work in the cane fields as labourers, using them as bodies to perform manual tasks, and ignoring their humanity. Later, films such as *White Zombie* (1932) expanded on this idea, with a sorceror named Murder Legendre employing armies of zombies to work in his factories. Thus, from its earliest origins, the zombie was identified as a human being who had been ruthlessly exploited, treated as a beast of burden, and made to suffer a life of pain and misery.

THE RAVAGING OF HAITI

From the fifteenth century on, Haiti, which was once inhabited by Taino Indians and boasted a wealth of mineral and other resources, was systematically ravaged by a succession of colonialist rulers, including the Spanish and French. Despite mounting the only successful slave uprising in history, which led to the establishment of the first black state, Haiti continued to be exploited by US and European interests, eventually succumbing to despotism by its own black rulers, under the Duvaliers. The Duvaliers introduced a horrific regime of military terrorism under their brutal army, the Tonton Macoutes. Taking advantage of the credulity of the uneducated population, Papa Doc Duvalier managed to persuade the masses that his henchmen were zombies, and that he was an African *loa*, namely Baron Samedi, guardian of the graveyard.

Looking at this history, we can see why the image of the zombie as the exploited labourer, with no prospect of living a decent human existence, deprived of a soul, of joy, of happiness, of everything that makes life worth living, became a potent one in Haitian culture. It told the story of the rape of a nation at the hands of greedy colonists and its own corrupt ruling class, reducing what was once a prosperous country rich in natural resources to a deforested, barren, poverty-stricken land.

THE HAITIAN EARTHQUAKE

Over time, Haiti became the poorest nation in the western hemisphere, its people left to suffer for the sins of its rulers in the past, defenceless against the storms and hurricanes that regularly battered the island. In January 2010, Haiti experienced one of the most devastating earthquakes in modern times. With its deforested hills, shanty towns, badly built cities, and minimal emergency services, it was in no position to withstand the devastation. Tens of thousands were killed.

ZOMBIES: ARE THEY REAL?

In the first two sections of this book, we look at the history of the Haitian zombie, from voodoo beliefs to modern anthropological studies, such as that of Wade Davies in his controversial account of the zombie myth, *The Serpent and the Rainbow*, published in 1985. We also discuss the zombie tales of early explorers such as the writer William Seabrook, whose travelogue *The Magic Island* appeared in 1945, and novelist Zora Neale Hurston, whose studies in black folklore included reports on the Haitian zombie. These writers raise the question of how much truth there is in the zombie myth: can human beings be paralysed so that they appear to be 'the living dead', or is the notion of a zombie simply a metaphor for the exploitation of poor farm labourers and peasants?

Here, we also discuss some of the alleged zombie sightings, such as the cases of Ti Joseph, Felicia Felix-Mentor and Clairvius Narcisse, and explore the secret societies of Haiti, known as Bisango.

THE HORROR ZOMBIE

We then move on to take a look at the modern horror zombie, on the face of it a very different being from the Haitian zombie of lore and legend. In 1968, filmmaker George Romero introduced a new type of zombie to the cinema screen, giving it a lurid 'horror' twist with lashings of gore, and focusing heavily on the reanimation aspect of the myth, in which dead bodies rise from the grave. Romero zombies, as they came to be called, were different from the Haitian zombie in that they lusted after human flesh, and were highly vicious, dangerous creatures who, though slow and lumbering, were unstoppable in their quest for live victims. They also differed from the monsters of European literature such as Frankenstein, since they were motivated entirely by the desire to feast on the living.

LUSTFUL GREED

In Romero's work, the zombie becomes a figure of death – rather like the hooded skeleton with the scythe – only the Romero zombie, instead of lingering in the shadows, bursts out of the graveyard and chases its victim. For Romero, death is always coming to get us, rather than waiting on the horizon. Thus,

his zombie figure expresses our fear of death as something about to engulf us, whether through disease, war, or apocalypse. The undead, for Romero, are always in hot pursuit of the living, not just lying in wait to claim their victims at the end.

This portrayal of determination, force and lustful greed on the part of the Romero zombie is light years away from the rather pathetic, passive image of the traditional Haitian zombie, labouring in the fields, a soulless shadow of its former self, bound into slavery for an evil tyrant of a master for the rest of its life. In a sense, the Romero zombie is rather more like the master of traditional Haitian folklore than the slave: a soulless, greedy consumer with no regard for the humanity of those whom he or she exploits. To

this degree, the Romero zombie is a parody of today's materialistic, shopping-fixated consumer. It is no accident that Romero set his 1974 movie *Dawn of the Dead* in a shopping mall, where the victims of the apocalypse barricade themselves in, surrounded by every conceivable luxury item but unable to escape, as they wait for the living dead to claim them.

THE ZOMBIE APOCALYPSE

Some horror zombie fans date the pre-Romero zombie films 'B.R.' (Before Romero) and the post-Romero ones 'A.R.' (After Romero). This is because it was Romero who ushered in a new archetype into the horror movie, and one that has been followed, with few significant alterations, ever since. Certainly, it is true to say that, over the decades since *Night of the Living Dead*, zombies have become faster and slicker: their slow, lumbering gait has been sped up, and their lust for blood has become more intense. However, the general themes raised in the film have persisted, including that of a modern zombie plague, or apocalypse.

Tales of a zombie or 'living dead' apocalypse take many forms, and have been a staple of film and literature for decades. It is, of course, the central element of many popular computer games, notably, *Resident Evil* and *Left 4 Dead*. These stories play on our fears for the future, our knowledge that our highly complex, sophisticated global civilisation has fundamental weaknesses, and may ultimately collapse, whether through war, natural disaster, or apparently man-made catastrophes such as global warming. The idea of the zombie apocalypse, a mass uprising of the nameless dead coming to claim us, is, of course, a very striking metaphor for this fear.

THE HORROR OF WAR

In addition, the concept of a zombie apocalypse addresses our sense of paranoia, our dread that in the modern world, with its relentless emphasis on consumerism and material success, the social bonds of respect, friendship and love between human beings may be broken. Thus, as well as standing for the inevitability of death, the zombie also expresses the individual's fear that a fellow human beings may turn out to be soulless automatons, devoid of feelings, sympathy or mercy.

Moreover, the notion of a zombie apocalypse is also, a rumination on the horror of war. Since the Vietnam War, which was raging in 1968 when Romero's *Night of the Living Dead* was made, the public has become accustomed to viewing news reports of horrific wars and atrocities on TV, in their living room. This, arguably, has created a somewhat blasé attitude to scenes of graphic violence. The horror zombie movie, to some extent, mirrors this thick-skinned attitude. However at the same time, one could also argue that Romero was seeking to bring the shock factor back into depictions of death and destruction, so as to remind us that loss of human life on a grand scale, as in war, is a terrible, dehumanising aspect of our modern civilisations.

THE FUTURE OF THE ZOMBIE

The exploitation of the labouring masses; the lust, greed and hunger of the consumer under modern capitalism; the soullessness of modern life; our fear of alienation from our fellow human beings; the horrors of war and mass atrocity; our anxiety about death and the vulnerability of the body: these are the themes that the zombie myth helps us to contemplate. But we should not forget that the zombie is also, first and foremost, a figure of fun: a big, shambling, dull-witted oaf, there to remind us that death, although horrific, can have a funny side. This is the message of such light-hearted horror comedies as *Shaun of the Dead* (2004), and the so-called 'zom rom coms' of modern fiction and cinema.

Clearly, the zombie myth has become well established in today's popular culture. On the one hand, it may be viewed as a morbid and tasteless trope; on the other, it may perhaps celebrate the fact that, although we can never outwit this figure of death entirely, as sentient human beings we have the upper hand for the time being. After all, we are the living, travelling towards the future; while the zombie, for all its fearsome gore, is essentially dead, a gruesome remnant of the past. Whichever view we take, the zombie looks set to take up permanent residence, along with vampires and werewolves, as one of the most popular figures in the contemporary horror pantheon.

ABOVE: Scene still from *Zombieland*, Ruben Fleischer, 2009.

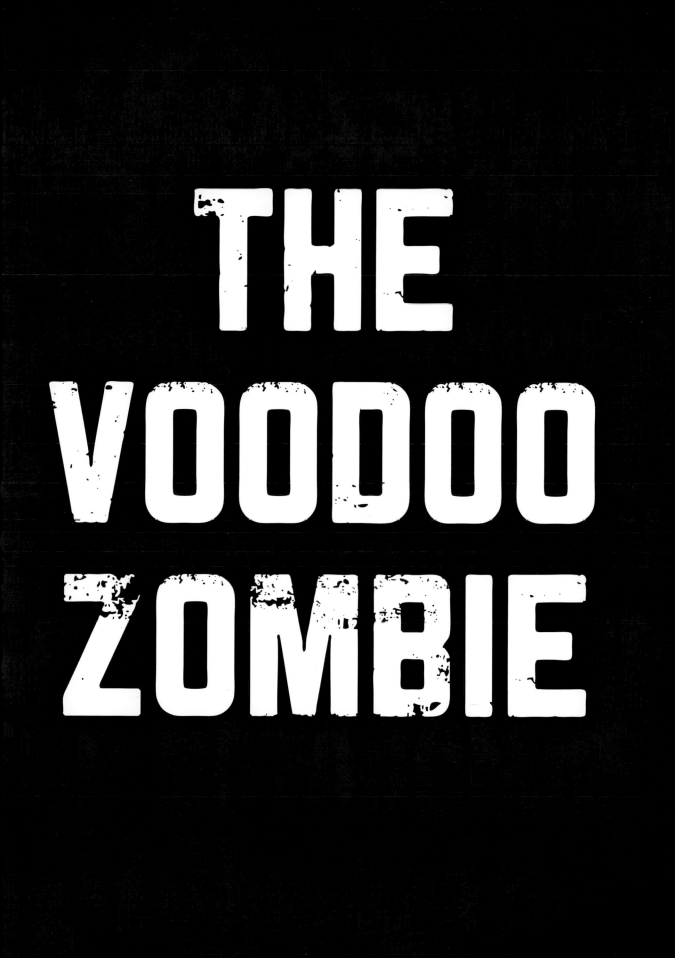

VODUN AND VOODOO

The ancient art of voodoo, which today is still practised in Haiti and other countries of the Caribbean, as well as parts of America, is a strange mixture of elements from different religions and cultures. It is essentially based on the West African religion of Vodun, which goes back thousands of years, and emphasises the importance of ancestors, whose wishes are interpreted by priests and priestesses attached to families or clans. However, it also incorporates elements of Roman Catholicism, which was mixed in with Vodun to disguise its African roots.

Slaves brought over from Africa to the Caribbean were prohibited by their white masters from practising their own religion, playing their own music or following their age-old rituals. The slave owners believed that keeping African culture alive would help to forge bonds between the slaves, which in turn might lead to revolution; they also viewed the slaves' culture and religious rituals as primitive and ungodly.

Despite being forced underground, the Vodun religion survived, amazingly enough, in a new, disguised form: Vodou, which became known in the popular media as voodoo. The religion was a combination of African Vodun, Roman Catholicism and certain aspects of Amerindian belief systems, particularly Arawak. In many ways, this new form of Vodun, transplanted into the New World by black slaves, was as spiritually profound and morally serious as Christianity and the other major faiths. (It was also extremely important to its followers, the slaves, who were suffering intense anguish as a result of being taken from their homelands, losing their liberty, and being treated as worthless.) However, over the years, it developed a reputation, mainly among white Americans and Europeans, as an evil form of witchcraft and sorcery. The darker, more disturbing aspects of the beliefs, rituals and icons of voodoo worship were emphasised to create a picture of an entirely menacing, sinister black art, rather than as a religion as insightful and complex as the ancient Greek or Roman systems of worship.

This new and evolved version of Vodun was contradictory in the sense that it held, on the one hand, polytheistic traits bearing remarkable resemblance to the ancient Greek and Roman religions

where its extended family of different gods controlled various aspects of life. However, through the influence of colonialists it now also had a central monotheistic vision of a distant ruling single god giving the religion a structural similarity to Christianity. Which is perhaps why it was relatively easy for the African slaves to switch from the loa of their ancient religion to the saints of the Roman Catholic church, who appeared to have much the same function.

A BLACK ART?

Over the centuries, Vodun became stigmatised as a black art and was driven underground, giving the religion a reputation as a secretive, malign type of sorcery practised among primitive black people. Some aspects of it, such as the belief that sorcerors could reanimate the dead, transforming them into mindless zombies to do their bidding, were exaggerated; while others, such as the use of voodoo dolls were wrongly described. In the Vodun religion, a doll symbolising, for instance, a sick person, is sometimes used in prayer. A name is pinned to the doll to direct the saint's attention to it, and so perhaps help ease his or her suffering. It is much more rare to find the doll being used malevolently, having pins stuck into it so as to bring harm or pain to the symbolised person.

In the same way, allegations of cannibalism and human sacrifice in the Vodun religion were largely exaggerated. Animal sacrifices were made on a regular basis, but in this respect, Vodun was not very different to the other major world religions, where such rituals had been a part of everyday worship since ancient times.

SEVERED LIMBS

Despite this, the Vodun religion as practised by black peoples in the Caribbean and the Americas became more and more sensationalised and vilified over the years. Violence, especially the cutting off of human limbs in order to make sacrifices and potions, and bizarre satanic rituals involving torture, were portrayed as the norm among its followers, which was very far from the truth. In 1884, a book by Spencer St John called *Haiti or the Black Republic* was published, giving lurid accounts of human sacrifice, torture and bloodletting as if these were everyday occurrences in the country. Naturally enough, with the

birth of the film industry not long afterwards, these stories caught the imagination of filmmakers and the 'horrors' of voodoo, as it came to be known, were further exaggerated in a series of early zombie movies. There was, of course, a hefty dose of racism in all this. Not only slave owners, but the general public, gave vent to their fear of cultural difference and their anxiety over maintaining their imperialist heritage by representing black people, and the Vodun religion, as brutal, bestial and inhuman. The reality was somewhat different, and those very same charges were later levelled at the imperialists, with good reason.

During the twentieth century, as the Vodun religion began to lose its spiritual roots and become commercialised as voodoo, there were those who tried to profit from the situation, peddling all manner of bogus spells, potions and trinkets. This trade became popular in Haiti and in New Orleans, where all sorts of scams took place, adding to the unsavoury reputation of voodoo. Voodoo came to be characterised as the belief system of a certain section of the Caribbean criminal underworld, where ruthlessness, brutality and greed ruled the day – a charge that was usually, but by no means always, unfair.

THE ROOTS OF VOODOO

The word *vodou* comes from an African word, *vodu*. In the Fon, Ewe and other languages it means spirit, but can also be translated as 'divine creation'. The Yoruba, Fon and Ewe peoples share a belief in a Creator, called Nana Buluku, and his two children, twins Lisa – god of the sun – and Mawu – goddess of the moon. Nana Buluku is a distant god who is not concerned with the details of human life, and thus leaves it to a host of vodou, or *orishas* – spiritual helpers who organise human affairs, such as protecting clans and ensuring their survival. These vodou spirits are grouped into families, and worshipped as ancestors, with priests and priestesses to serve them.

In the Vodun religion, there are many deities connected with the natural world, such as *mami wata*, water gods and goddesses who rule the seas and rivers, and *sakpata*, who are in charge of disease and illness. In addition, some gods

supervise human occupations and attributes; for instance, Ogoun, or Gu, rules the world of blacksmiths and ironworkers, while Legba, also known as Eshu, is a messenger deity known for his cleverness and wily ways. The African Eshu, who is responsible for maintaining a balance between the spirit and human worlds, is quite often depicted as a young, stocky man carrying a large stick. In contrast, his later incarnation as Papa Legba in Caribbean voodoo, he is seen as an elderly man with a crutch.

DRIED ANIMAL PARTS

There are a wide variety of rituals, songs and dances to praise the gods, but generally it is common among the worshippers to sacrifice animals as a way of thanking or appeasing the gods. A number of talismans, or fetishes are also used to maintain contact with the spirit world, to heal, and to bring back youth and vigour. These are often dried animal parts, but may also be small statues. Another belief is that departed ancestors coexist with the living. Women are organised into groups, with a Mama, or Queen Mother, at the head. As well as attending to practical duties such as administering the buying and selling of food at markets, the Queen Mothers lead their communities in prayer, and in times gone by, would pray for the safe return of men from the clan who had gone to fight tribal wars. The women often wielded great power among their peoples, a feature of social coordination that was later kept alive among the slaves of the Caribbean and the southern states of America.

THE SORCERORS

As mentioned above, the evil nature of Vodun has been greatly exaggerated over the centuries, often as a way of rationalising the suppression of this religion, and forcing it underground. However, it must be said that there is, as in most religions, a dark side to Vodun. Vodun followers believe in the power of sorcerors, known as *botono* or *azeto*. These mysterious and highly respected figures were said to be able to summon up the spirits and cause their opponents – whether individuals or whole communities – harm through magic spells and rituals. They were also credited with the power to reanimate the dead, making them their slaves for life (see page 41). This is where the notion of the zombie began, and though it forms part of the general belief system of Vodun, it is by no means central to it.

VODUN TODAY

The roots of the Vodun religion date back over six thousand years, and it established itself across a large swathe of Africa, chiefly in what was then called Dahomey (now Benin), and also in parts of Nigeria and Togo. During the period of colonial rule, efforts were made to stamp out the religion, but it survived underground, in secret orders which continued to worship the gods. Later, during the Marxist regime of Benin from 1975 to 1989, the religion was again banned, but with the establishment of a democratic government in 1991, Vodun was once again permitted as a form of worship.

In 1996 it became the official religion of the country.

Today, Vodun is practised by millions of people across the world, not only in Benin, but in Haiti, the Dominican Republic, Ghana, Togo and parts of the USA. In Africa, South America and the Caribbean, there are a number of religions with features similar to Vodun, including Candoble, Santeria Lucumi, Macumba, Quimbanda and Umbanda.

THE LOA

In recent times, rather than demonising Vodun, commentators have tended to point to the similarities between this ancient African religion and aspects of Christian belief. Both teach that there is a Creator and an afterlife. The African *loa*, or spirits, have a similar function to the Christian saints, and in many cases are conceived of as exceptional individuals who, after their death, go on to supervise particular areas of human society and occupations. In addition, Vodun worshippers believe in a special, personal *loa* who looks after them, similar to a patron saint or guardian angel.

There is also a similarity between Vodun and Christianity in that both believe in the existence of evil, and of the devil, or demons. At certain points in history, this aspect of Christianity is emphasised, while at others, it is downplayed – medieval Christians for example, had a vivid sense of the demon world, in the same way that Vodun worshippers continue to have.

HAITIAN VODOU

This religion, also known as *sevis lwa* (service to the loa) is a mixture of African Vodun and Roman Catholicism, which dates from the sixteenth century, when the first slaves were brought over from Africa to the Caribbean. The slaves were impelled to convert to Christianity, but instead of leaving their traditional religion behind, they simply included it in their new belief system. Today, Vodou is still an important part of the culture of Haiti, and related forms exist in parts of the Caribbean and South America.

In this way, Vodou – a 'syncretic' religion made up of two or more previously separate belief systems – was born. It originated from the island of Hispaniola, where many slaves were taken, and which later became partitioned as Haiti and the Dominican Republic.

In Haitian Vodou, The Creator is called *Bondye* which is derived from the French for good God, *Bon Dieu*. The African *loa* spirits from Vodun become *lwa* – the most important being *Papa Legba* who guards the spiritual crossroads of life, allowing human beings to speak to God, and bringing messages from God to the people. Other spirits include *Kouzin Zaka*, the spirit of farming; *Erzulie Fred*, the spirit of love; and *Simbi*, the spirit of rain. According to Vodou lore, the many spirits divide into twenty-one nations, some of which war with each other. For example, the hot-blooded *Petwo* nation conflicts with the *Rada* nation, which is calmer. They are further divided into families who rule over various aspects of life, including fertility, death, farming and war. Each of the lwa has a connection with a particular Roman Catholic saint, in a complex system that may include many deities. For example, *Li Grand Zombi*, the snake deity, has a special relationship with St Patrick, who was well known in Catholic teachings for his power to cast out snakes.

In a particular household, shrines are set up for ancestors and spirits, with special foods, scents, candles, flowers and drinks displayed. On a certain spirit's 'day', candles are lit, Catholic 'Hail Marys' and 'Our Fathers' recited, Papa Legba acknowledged, and then the individual spirit addressed through prayers.

DIVINE POSSESSION

Despite its links with Roman Catholicism, the communal form of service in Haitian Vodou is quite different from that of the Christian church. Before the service, large quantities of food – especially chicken – are cooked, and altars set up. Services are conducted by a *Houngan* – a priest – or a *Mambo* – a priestess, and vary according to their particular taste and characteristics. The service begins with French songs and Catholic prayers, and then there is a roll-call of all the saints worshipped by that community, both African and Roman Catholic. Prayers are offered up to the saints, called *Priye Gine*, or African Prayer, and the spirit of the drums, *Hounto*, is invoked to help with the festivities.

As with the Pentecostalists, Vodou worshippers believe that when they pray, the spirit may enter an individual, and speak through them. When this happens, the Vodouisants, as the worshippers are called, believe themselves to be very lucky, and expect good fortune to come upon their households. During the night, there may be many such possessions, and often the celebration becomes quite informal and quite chaotic, as the participants discuss which songs

and prayers should be performed. Arguments can also break out over whether the Houngan or Mambo is enabling or obstructing the descent of the spirits to the *bossale* – the uninitiated worshippers.

TERRORIST DEATH SQUADS

Over the years, Vodou in Haiti became a centre of resistance to European imperialism. Missionaries were constantly sent to the island to try to convert the slaves, but they failed. The Haitians continued to worship their gods as they saw fit, despite intense pressure to drop the *sevis lwa* that connected them to their African forefathers.

In 1791, a slave revolt in Haiti began with a Vodou ceremony known as *Bwa Kayiman*, in which a black pig was sacrificed to the spirit Ezili Dantor, and the worshippers – African captives from over twenty different nations – listened to Voudon priest, Papaloi Boukman, preach about the need for revolution against the cruel slave drivers who were making their lives hell. After a long, hard struggle, the Haitian people threw off French colonial rule in 1804, becoming the first black people's republic to do so. As the first independent nation of the Americas, and the only nation whose independence was gained as the result of a slave rebellion, it became a beacon of hope for other states and countries struggling against European oppression.

Sadly, however, in the years that followed, the country deteriorated as a series of invaders, beginning with Napoleon Bonaparte, attempted to re-take the island. From 1915 to 1934, under US occupation, the constitutional system was dismantled, forced labour reintroduced and the population subjugated. Later, under the rule of the Duvalier family, the Haitians suffered from a totalitarian regime which included terrorist death squads known as Tonton Macoutes. Many fled the country, leaving their compatriots to suffer poverty, disease and misery under a series of unstable governments. Today, Haiti is one of the poorest and least developed countries in the world, with over eighty per cent of the population living in poverty as small-scale subsistence farmers.

SCAMS AND CORRUPTION

Not surprisingly, in this situation of political corruption, social destabilisation and extreme poverty, the Vodou religion, along with other aspects of Haitian life, also deteriorated. Vodou began to be exploited by unscrupulous Houngans and Mambos, who began to demand huge sums of money for their services. These priests were regarded as powerful people, who had the opportunity to make a large income, and so many joined the order simply to line their own pockets. In this way, true Vodou began to die out, replaced by a commercial version of the religion that centred on extracting as much money as possible from naïve and desperate inhabitants of the island as well as credulous tourists, rather than serving the spirits. Various scams were concocted to fleece the victims, and the importance of the more lurid aspects of the religion stepped up.

These included ideas about zombies and voodoo dolls, which are not intrinsic to the Vodou religion or to the priests, but which are the preserve of the *bokor*, the sorcerer, having a basis in non-religious folklore.

THE VOODOO DOLL

In Haiti, there is a practice of nailing small wooden dolls and old shoes onto trees near a cemetery, in the belief that these little dolls will bear a message from the living to the spirit world. In addition, plastic dolls are sometimes used on home-made altars to honour the spirits. Such dolls, and other power objects, are known as *pwen*, and are comparable to the holy objects, or *nkisi*, of parts of Africa. However, they are regarded as having power in themselves, and are not seen as substitutes for a person – in fact, the practice of sticking pins in a doll representing a particular person in order to harm them, appears to derive from European folk magic. Nevertheless, the idea of the Haitian voodoo doll has persisted, and these objects are now sold as souvenirs to tourists who visit the country.

NEW ORLEANS VOODOO

As the Vodun religion spread to different parts of the Americas, so the slave communities that worshipped it developed varying

traditions in their belief systems and forms of reverence. In addition, these variations became mixed up with local folklore, creating a hybrid of religious belief and heathen superstition. In New Orleans, where enormous numbers of African slaves were taken to the slave market to be sold, the tradition came to be known as voodoo and began to incorporate elements of folklore as well as religious belief. A system of occult magic and paraphernalia, called *hoodoo*, was developed, which emphasised the importance of Li Grand Zombi, the snake deity from the Congo, and of the power of the *gris gris*, a Wolof (a language of Western Africa) term for a talisman that is thought to bring luck and protect the wearer from harm. These terms were later introduced to the American public through popular cultural forms such as blues music, and through many novels and films. Thus it was, along with stories of secret Satanic rituals and practices, that the idea arose that voodoo was a form of devil worship practised by black people, particularly African Americans in the South.

Among their panoply of occult objects was the *ouanga*, a charm bag that contained items such as herbs, poisonous dried roots and ground-up bones. This was designed to poison or bring harm to enemies. Another item was the *mojo*, made of red flannel cloth, tied with a drawstring, and containing dried animal parts, plants, shells and inscriptions on papers. The mojo would be worn under clothing, and was thought to be particularly effective in matters of romance, lending the wearer the skill to attract the opposite sex

and impress as a powerful lover. A *grimoire*, or magic textbook, was also used to give instructions as to how to cast magic spells, invoke angels and demons, foresee the future, and make talismans. Finally, there was the *gris gris*, which, like the mojo, was said to enhance a lover's power, and aid lovemaking.

VOODOO QUEENS

Another aspect of the tradition specific to New Orleans was the rise of the voodoo queens. These bearers of magic became powerful figures in the black community and beyond: one of them, Marie Laveau, was reputed to have over 10,000 followers, both black and white, who regularly attended her rituals on St John's Eve at the Bayou St John. Her fame and influence were legendary in nineteenth-century New Orleans, though today much of her life is shrouded in mystery. She is reputed to have run a brothel, and for a period, kept a boa constrictor, named Li Grand Zombi, as her pet. Her daughter, also named Marie Laveau, continued to ply the voodoo trade after her death.

As with Haitian Vodou, New Orleans voodoo became heavily commercialised, as unscrupulous practitioners began to sell mojos, gris gris, and other forms of voodoo medicine to credulous customers. Spells and hexes were bought and sold at exploitative rates, so much so that today, a great deal of the tradition's spiritual depth has been lost.

HAITIAN VODOU

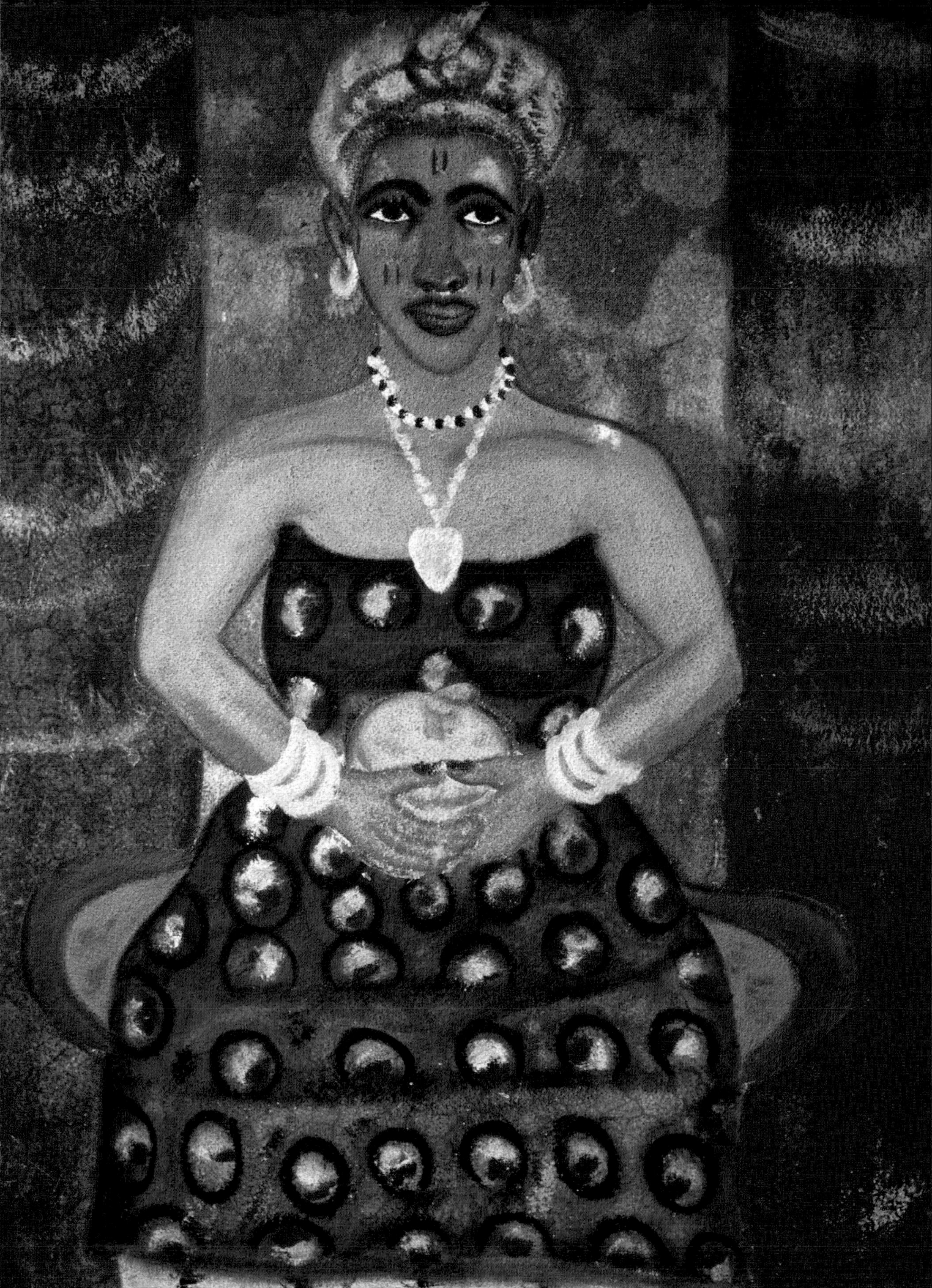

VOODOO & NECROMANCY

As well as having roots in the ancient African religion of Vodun, voodoo draws inspiration from the European tradition of necromancy. Necromancy is the practice of calling up dead spirits for the purposes of prophecy. There are many methods of doing this, some of them fairly innocuous – such as trying to contact a dead person in a séance – and others extremely unpleasant – such as exhuming corpses and performing various grisly rites upon them. Not surprisingly necromancy has been frowned upon from earliest times as 'the blackest of the black arts'.

At various periods in history, it has been banned as an evil form of witchcraft, and continues to be viewed by the Catholic church as a form of demoniacal superstition. However, despite opposition both from church and state, necromancy has persisted up to the present day, and continues to be widely practised in the African religion of Quimbanda and, to a lesser degree, its spiritual cousins, Santeria and Voodoo.

THE BLACK ARTS

The word necromancy means prophecy of the dead: from the Greek *nekros* – dead – and *manteia* – prophecy or divination. In the Middle Ages, the word was altered to *nigromancy*, meaning the black arts, and began to lose its specific meaning of summoning the dead for advice, help and counsel. There was a belief, at this period, that spirits of the dead could only be summoned with the help of a Christian priest, who could call upon God to aid the process, and who had knowledge of demonology – the study of demons and evil supernatural beings from a Christian point of view. (Within Christian theology, there are early texts, such as that of the thirteenth-century priest Thomas Aquinas, that give specific instructions on how to deal with demons.) Because of this, many priests became involved in the black arts, especially necromancy, performing all kinds of horrific rituals with dead bodies, so much so, that the Church finally banned this practice as witchcraft, punishable by death and imprisonment. However, the phenomenon of priests dabbling in the black arts did not entirely cease. After all, as regards demons, the medieval priests shared a similar world view to those who relied on magic, folklore and superstition to guide them: the medieval Christian, like the pagan, believed in evil spirits and the ability of priests and witches to harness their power through incantation, ritual and sorcery.

DESCENT INTO THE UNDERWORLD

Necromancy has been practised, in many cultures, from ancient times, usually involving the idea that a dead spirit, if summoned, can enter and possess an individual, who will then speak with the dead person's voice to the assembled company. The Greek geographer Strabo refers to necromancy as the main form of prophecy among the Persians, while in Babylon there were reports of necromancers, known as *Manzanu*, who raised spirits they called *Etemmu*.

In most cultures, there is an idea that in order to raise the dead, one has to descend into the underworld, which is necessarily a voyage fraught with danger and holds many terrors – the worst of which, is being unable to return to the land of the living. In Egyptian legend, we find the story of Isis, who descends into the underworld to find the dead Osiris and bring him back to life, while in Greek literature, Homer tells the story of Odysseus, who makes a journey into Hades and tries to revive the prophet Tiresias by casting spells he has learned from the goddess Circe. He has to conduct his rituals at night, around a firepit, offering blood from sacrificial animals for the ghost to drink.

> many priests became involved in the black arts, performing all kinds of horrific rituals with dead bodies

THE BONE CONJURORS

In the Bible, there are many warnings against necromancy. The Book of Deuteronomy, warns the Israelites against using this Canaanite practice, and in the Book of Samuel we read of King Saul, who asked the Witch of Endor to raise the ghost of the prophet Samuel for him, because he needed his help. Unfortunately, the reply from Samuel's ghost was rather negative; King Saul was told off for dabbling in the black arts, and predicted that he would lose a major battle the following day. Perhaps demoralised, Saul went on to be defeated in battle, and afterwards killed himself.

Despite these dire warnings about raising the dead, we ironically find two important stories in the Bible in which this very process is seen as sacred and holy. The first is the story of the raising of Lazarus, and the second a central theme of the Christian religion – the raising of Jesus from the tomb after his crucifixion, and his ascent into heaven with the words: 'I am the resurrection and the life. He that believes in me will live, even though he dies; and whoever lives and believes in me will never die'. Christian theology appears to take the view that, when the dead are raised by ordinary human beings using sorcery, without the blessing of God, this is wholly evil; but when God intervenes, as in the case of Jesus and Lazarus, we have borne witness to a divine miracle. Significantly, an aspect of Judaic lore is taken into the Christian story of the resurrection: it is a woman, Mary Magdalene, who aids in the process. Some theologians have argued that the Jews may have taken particular exception to the Christian teaching of the resurrection precisely because it conflicted with the Judaic prohibition against raising the dead.

DEMONIC MAGIC

From the late fifteenth to the early eighteenth century, moral panic about necromancy and the black arts reached a peak of hysteria. Women, often childless older women previously thought of as wise and knowledgeable about folklore (akin to shamans), began to be targeted, along with the priests, as potential sources of evil. They were excluded from society, hunted down, and put to death in a variety of horrifying ways: by drowning, burning, mutilation and torture. During this period, it is estimated that about one hundred thousand women lost their lives in this way. Historians have linked the medieval witch-hunts to economic and spiritual collapse after the Black Death (bubonic plague), but there was also a fear that older, independent women were a threat to the social order and were persecuted for this reason.

In 1485, one of the first books to be printed on the newly invented printing press was a manual for witch-hunting produced by the Catholic authorities. The *Malleus Maleficarum*, otherwise known as *The Hammer of the Witches*, contained the following description of women:

> *All wickedness is as nothing compared to the wickedness of woman. What else is woman but a foe to friendship, an unescapable punishment, a necessary evil, a natural temptation, a desirable calamity, domestic danger, a delectable detriment, an evil nature, painted with fair colours. ... Women are by nature instruments of*

Satan – they are by nature carnal, a structural defect rooted in the original creation.

No wonder the book was described as a work of deranged misogyny.

Ironically, mass hysteria about the black arts, driven by the Catholic church, actually had the effect of keeping it alive. The church, by reacting to witchcraft with such moral panic and vicious brutality, ensured that successive generations came to believe in the power of sorcery. Necromancy, in particular, became much more central to the belief system of ordinary people than it would have done had the practice been quietly ignored.

MUTILATION OF CORPSES

In medieval times, necromancers were able to ply a bustling trade in rituals and relics, with a stream of credulous customers beating a path to their doors. Necromancers engaged in rituals involving magic circles, incantations, wands, bells and various talismans. They surrounded themselves with deathly objects, such as skulls and bones, and often took to wearing dead people's clothing, so as to help summon the spirits. In addition, they might have eaten a diet of black food, including unfermented grape juice and unleavened black bread, symbols of lifeless inertia. Sometimes they would visit graveyards to exhume a body, mutilate it, and even, in some cases, eat parts of it. They may have also performed these same rituals on recently deceased corpses who had not yet been buried. Such rituals might last for days or weeks.

The rituals often took the form of Christian exorcism, with prayers, incense and chanting, but there were also Arab influences in the astral magic that the necromancers used, concerning phases of the moon, the planets and the position of the sun.

Christian clergy also indulged in this popular but very secret activity of summoning the dead. Many priests had a side job in performing rituals associated with the occult. In order to help them perform their exorcisms, they would often revert to studying magic and the black arts, despite the fact that this was expressly forbidden by the authorities.

MIND CONTROL

The purpose of necromancy was to overpower another's will, to perform magic tricks and to gain knowledge. The necromancers believed that through their rituals and secret lore, they could enter the mind of another human being and force him or her to do their bidding. (This aspect of necromancy is particularly relevant to the concept of the zombie in West Indian folklore, as we shall see later.) The necromancers were also thought to be capable of inducing death, disease and destruction on certain individuals; summoning demons to drive people mad, to inflame their passions, or to engage in evil deeds. In addition, they were said to have the power to conjure up practical items, such as food and means of transport, to help them in their endeavours. Finally, they were able to use the demons' knowledge to help them track down a criminal, or, in some cases, foresee the future.

HOODOO

Connected to the practice of voodoo is a set of beliefs, practises and rituals known as hoodoo. It draws on elements from many different types of folklore, including African, Native American and European. It is based around beliefs and customs from the West and Central African religion of Vodun, and the related religion from the Caribbean and New Orleans, Vodou, but within it there are also aspects of Native American plant lore, as well as a strong element of the European black arts.

Most hoodoo practitioners are African Americans, but since the nineteenth century, when the term became widely known, there have been a sizeable number of white American followers as well.

The practice is known, in different regions, by various names: *hoodoo*, *conjure*, *conjuration*, *tricking*, and *rootwork*. The term rootwork refers to the central practice of making potions, casting spells and fashioning charms from dried roots. However, rootworkers may limit themselves to botanical knowledge only, and may reject general hoodoo concepts and beliefs.

THE HOODOO DOCTOR

In some rural areas of the US, hoodoo is also known by the common catch-all term witchcraft, but this can be misleading. It is certainly true that hoodoo does rely on one central aspect of the European tradition of witchcraft – namely the use of grimoires, however, it has little to do with European pagan religions such as Wicca, which is also known as witchcraft.

Indeed, the word hoodoo is often used very loosely, to describe the practice of making magic, a magician, or a particular type of magic. It arose among African slaves in the southern states of the United States, and developed over the centuries in piecemeal fashion. As a result, it has no formal structure, and is usually practised by lay people, often within a Christian framework. In the past, the hoodoo doctor would be a nomad, travelling from town to town selling charms, potions and spells. Alternatively, he or she might be a recognised and respected figure among the community, being called in to help with such issues as sickness, love problems or disputes.

AN EYE FOR AN EYE

Hoodoo highlights the personal magic power of the practitioner, so consequently there is no hierarchy of priests, priestesses, initiates and laity. Traditionally, knowledge was passed on from person to person, through families and social contacts, but from the nineteenth century, it began to be written down and disseminated in books. Today, hoodoo scholarship and the marketing of hoodoo 'spiritual services' flourishes on the internet.

In most versions of the practice, there is a belief in the Old Testament teaching of 'an eye for an eye, a tooth for a tooth', namely, that our misdeeds will rebound on us, and that we will eventually suffer the same cruelty that we mete out to our enemies. Thus, if a hoodoo magician casts a spell to cause the death of a murderer, this is seen as acceptable, since it is a form of retribution. The New Testament teaching of 'turning the other cheek', that is, forgiving our enemies for their misdeeds instead of repeating them, is not, in most cases, part of the hoodoo world view.

MOSES THE MAGICIAN

Within the hoodoo belief system, the Christian Bible is seen as the ultimate grimoire, which may impart secrets and spells to those who can decipher its true meaning. The Book of Genesis, with its story of how the world was made, is seen as proof that God is the ultimate conjuror, able to create an entire planet in a matter of days. Other biblical figures, such as Moses, are viewed as tremendously powerful hoodoo magicians, receiving information direct from God, such as the ten commandments, and able to perform magic tricks and miracles, such as turning a staff into a snake. Significantly, in the context of African slavery, Moses was seen as the supreme conjuror, with the power to lead his people, the Israelites, out of bondage.

Thus, hoodoo practitioners began to scan the Bible for clues as to how to cast spells, in the hope that they could find a way out of their servitude. Over the years, however, when it became clear that no miracle would free the slaves of their bonds, their study became more pragmatic, and instead, they became a port of call for those suffering particular problems. The hoodoo doctors began to consult reference works such as *Secrets of the Psalms*, which purported to show how to use the biblical psalms to ensure, for instance, successful partnerships, safe travel and good health.

THE 'DARK MAN'

Another little known aspect of hoodoo is the incorporation of elements of the Kaballah, a very ancient, esoteric school of thought within Judaism. The aim of Kaballah is to explore the relationship between the Creator and the mortal world, and help individuals to spiritual realisation. During the nineteenth century, a number of grimoires professing to be based on the Kaballah began to circulate in Europe, notably one text called *The Sixth and Seventh Book of Moses*. This contained signs, seals and spells that were apparently used by Moses to perform miracles. In addition, a spell book known as *Pow Wows* was published in 1820 and promised not only to impart arcane biblical knowledge, but to protect the bearer from harm: 'Whoever carries this book with him is safe from all his enemies, visible or invisible; and whoever has this book with him cannot die... nor drown in any water, nor burn up in any fire, nor can any unjust sentence be passed upon him.' Clearly, the marketing device worked, and the book became a central text in the armory of hoodoo magic.

As well as God, Moses and other biblical figures, the hoodoo practitioner also relies on the power of an African deity, known by various names including *Eshu* or *Legba*. In the Vodun religion (see page 20), this figure takes messages from the Creator to the human world. In hoodoo, he becomes a 'dark man' at the crossroads, a trickster, akin to a pagan devil or demon. However, he is not to be confused with the biblical Satan, as although he can be a difficult and demanding deity, he is not evil, and contrary to much popular belief, hoodoo is not devil worship. It is perhaps more akin to the ancient belief systems that emphasise the capriciousness of the gods, and how they must be cajoled and appeased in order that they might look benevolently on the world of obscure human beings.

BODILY FLUIDS

The overall goal of hoodoo is to persuade the various supernatural spirits to help particular individuals with pressing problems in their lives, whether to do with money, love, health or employment – prayers are made, spells cast, love potions administered and medicinal potions advised. As in many other cultures, use is made of plants, especially herbs, semi-precious stones, animal parts and possessions of sentimental value. There is also a belief in the magical power of human bodily fluids such as blood – especially menstrual blood – semen and urine, which are often used in making potions and poultices. In early times, these hoodoo products would be home-made, but in the early twentieth century, commercial companies began to make and sell them, advertising them as 'spiritual supplies'. Today, there continues to be a healthy trade in such hoodoo items as magic crystals, roots, herbs, candles, incense, household cleaning products, bath salts and colognes.

The various types of hoodoo spells include many forms of revenge magic in which evildoers, or enemies, are punished. In *foot track magic*, the hoodoo doctor attempts to harness the magical essence of a person's footprint. Dirt from the footprint may be bottled to make a spell and buried where the victim will step over it. In addition 'hot foot powder' may be sprinkled across the person's path, which, when he or she treads on it, will cause all manner of bad luck. Another form of foot track magic includes crossing a person's path with a mark, or with powders and herbs, so that they may experience bad luck for a number of years. In order to ward off the effects of foot track magic, individuals may wear special amulets, such as silver dimes, wash their floors with hoodoo preparations, and wear leaves or twigs from the devil's shoe string plant in their shoes. This plant is said to tie down the devil, and make it impossible for him to do harm.

'LOVE ME OIL'

Other items in the hoodoo doctor's bag of tricks include an indigenous American plant called John the Conqueror Root, which is also used extensively in Native American folkore for medicinal and magical purposes. The hoodoo doctor also sells the Mojo Hand, a flannel bag filled with items such as roots, stones and herbs. This bag is thought to ward off bad luck, and can be worn, or stashed where the owner lives or works. According to hoodoo belief, no one else must touch this bag, otherwise dreadful harm may ensue.

As well as the Mojo Hand, some hoodoo followers use the luck ball, a hidden object wound with string, or a black hen's egg, an egg that is filled with magic powders. Sachets containing magic powders are also popular, and may have such colourful names as Kiss Me Now, Follow Me Boy, Love Me Oil, Law Keep Away and Money Stay with Me.

ZOMBIE SPIRIT BOTTLE

The spirit bottle can be traced back to ninth-century Congo, where blue bottles would be hung on trees to catch the light. It was believed that the dazzling light from the bottles would attract spirits, who would enter the bottle and become trapped. When, in the seventeenth century, African slaves were brought to the Americas in large numbers, they brought this tradition with them, and many years later, the idea found its way into hoodoo as the zombie spirit bottle.

The hoodoo doctor may prescribe the zombie spirit bottle to bring good fortune and to keep harm away. This is a small bottle in which, according to hoodoo legend, the spirit of a zombie is kept, captured through ritual spells and incantations. The person who owns this bottle can command the spirit to do his or her bidding. The zombie spirit must be kept happy with offerings of spicy food and rum, and in return will perform many years of faithful service. However, if the spirit grows unhappy, which can be determined by sighs coming from the bottle, the spirit must be set free. The bottle must be broken, and the pieces buried at a crossroads or in a graveyard.

THE BOKOR

The *bokor* is a powerful, sinister figure in the Vodou religion. He is distinct from the *houngan*, or priest, in that he practises the black arts, which includes the creation of *ouangas* and *wangas* – talismans and charms that house spirits: the ouanga, for the purposes of doing good; and the wanga, to bring bad luck.

There are many Haitian folk tales about the bokor, whose doings are shrouded in mystery, and whose powers are respected and feared. The most disturbing of these is that the bokor can create zombies ...

Whether or not the bokor can be completely disassociated from the houngan is debatable. As in the Christian religion, where medieval priests sometimes dabbled in the black arts, so the houngan may 'serve the *lwa* with both hands' – meaning, that he may practise both black magic and white magic. Indeed, some regard the bokor and the houngan as interchangeable figures, with a multitude of functions within the community, including acting as priests, doctors and mediums, bringing messages from and to the spirit world.

STEALING SOULS

In Haitian Vodou, the soul is conceived of as a dual entity, with two guardian angels presiding over it: the *gro bonanj* and the *ti bonanj*. The *gro bonanj*, which represents the individual's conscious being, migrates after death to join the world of the lwa, residing there until he or she too becomes a lwa. Meanwhile, the *ti bonanj*, which represents the individuality or will of that particular human being, remains. It is this that the bokor seeks to capture, stealing it away so that the person left has no personality or will, and lives a deadened life without a soul.

> the soul is conceived of as a dual entity, with two guardian angels presiding over it

Traditionally, those who undergo zombification are people who have sinned, particularly those who have committed crimes against the whole community. Such individuals may be punished by the bokor by being transformed into zombies, to live out the rest of their lives as his slaves. In this way, sinners are believed to atone for their past misdeeds, by being condemned to a life in death, as a member of the 'walking dead'.

THE CREATION OF ZOMBIES

There are various methods that the bokor uses to create zombies. The first, and perhaps most sinister, is to use a potion to drug the live individual, reducing them to a vegetative state. Traditionally, the potion contains a poison called tetrodotoxin, extracted from the pufferfish, one of the most poisonous vertebrates in the world. The effects of this are numbing of the tongue and lips, vomiting and dizziness, and then paralysis of the entire body, increasing the heart rate and lowering blood pressure. The drug also causes severe neurological damage, mostly affecting the left side of the brain, which controls memory, speech and motor skills. The victim appears to stop breathing, and the pulse lowers to the point that it is hard to detect. If the poison is administered in the right dosage, a coma will ensue for several days, during which time the victim may be fully conscious, but unable to speak or move. If too much poison is given, the victim's diaphragm muscles will become paralysed, causing death by suffocation.

THE COUP PADRE

The poison is prepared with a concoction of mystical herbs, human and animal parts, including blood and hair. Voodoo dolls and fetishes may also be part of the ritual. The mixture is sometimes brewed up and given to a victim to drink, or it may be given as a powder. In some instances, it is thought to be injected by blow dart. This fatal dose is known as the *coup padre*, and has the instant effect of rendering the victim immobile within seconds. This comatose state persists so long that the victim is presumed dead, taken to the morgue and then buried. The horrifying aspect of this is that, according to legend, victims may be fully conscious during the whole process, but unable to speak or move a muscle to alert anyone to his or her true condition.

REANIMATION

Once the body has been buried, the bokor's evil plan becomes clear. The bokor will visit the graveyard, usually at night, exhume the corpse and perform a variety of ancient voodoo rites on the body, designed to take possession of the victim's soul, or ti bonanj. The bokor traps this soul in a small clay jar, wrapping it with one of the victim's personal possessions, such as a piece of jewellery or a fragment of clothing, and hides it away in a secret place. The soul is replaced by a lwa controlled by the bokor, and in this way, the victim becomes the slave of the bokor, unable to think or feel, but simply the blind servant of his master.

After this ceremony, two or more days elapse, and the bokor is ready to reanimate his victim. This is done by administering *Datura stramonium*, a plant known in Haiti as zombie's cucumber.

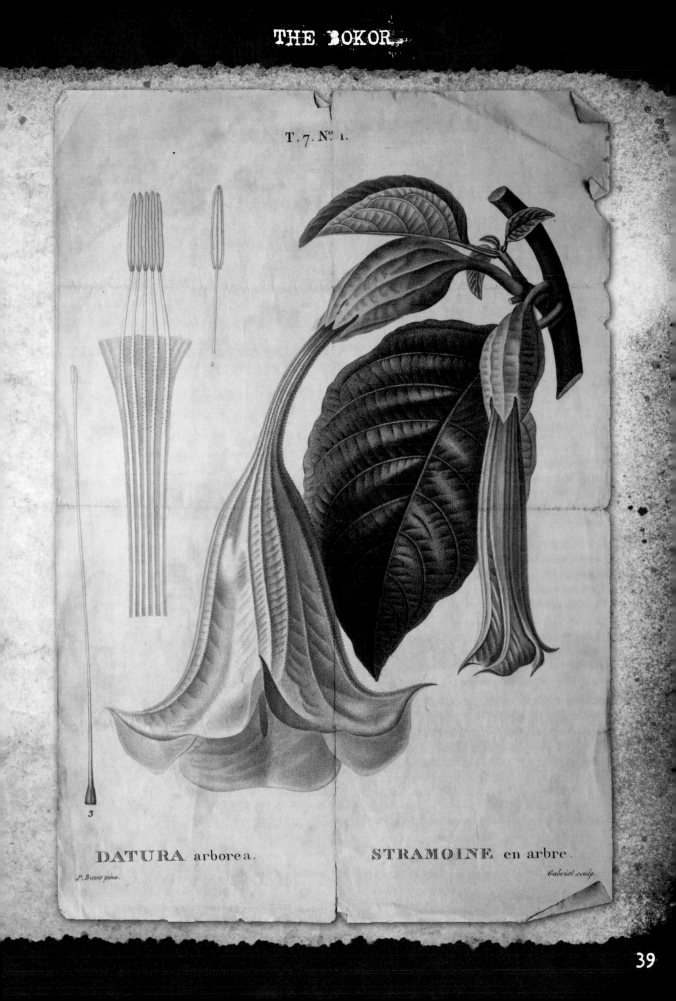

T. 7. N.º 1.

DATURA arborea. STRAMOINE en arbre.

P. Bessa pinx. Gabriel sculp.

ZOMBIE'S CUCUMBER

The zombie's cucumber belongs to the *Datura* genus, a species of toxic plants that have trumpet-shaped flowers. For centuries, they have been known to cause delirious states as well as death, and are regarded in the same light as well-known poisonous plants and herbs such as henbane, mandrake and deadly nightshade, which have been used by sorcerors and witches to create poisonous brews and love potions.

Datura has a variety of evocative common names, including Angel's Trumpet, Hell's Bells, Jimson Weed and Gypsum Weed. It is common in Central America, where it was used by Native Americans of certain tribes to initiate boys into manhood. In India, where it also grows, it was used by Hindu *sadhus* – holy men – who smoked it with cannabis in order to have mystical visions. It played a part in the history of America, when in 1607, starving settlers attempted to eat the plants, repeatedly boiling them to rid them of their toxic properties. They escaped death, but were reputed to have been dazed for several days while the drug took its effects. In 1676, *Datura* figured again in the annals of American history, when soldiers attempted to suppress an uprising in the Bacon's Rebellion. The soldiers were drugged with the weed, either accidentally or through a plot, and instead of fighting the rebels, were seen dancing about

> holy men smoked it with cannabis in order to have mystical visions

making monkey faces, chasing feathers, and generally acting in a deranged fashion.

Later, around the turn of the twentieth century, *stramonium* was extracted from the plant and used in medicine as daturine to treat bronchial spasm in asthmatics. The leaf was made into cigarettes which were smoked by the patient to relax the bronchial tubes, or alternatively, burned in an open dish, along with cannabis, for the patient to inhale. Daturine was also used to calm patients suffering from mania, and as a sleeping draught. However, the toxic effects of the plant were later deemed too dangerous to continue this practice, and today it is banned for medicinal use.

A LIVING DREAM

Datura is described as creating the effect of living in a dream, and may be so strong that it causes permanent psychological damage. This is because the hallucinations that are experienced seem as real as everyday events. Instead of sensory distortions, as caused by magic mushrooms or LSD, the effect of *Datura* is to conjure up unreal experiences, which may be completely ordinary, such as smoking a cigarette, going for a walk or making a cup of tea, but which are purely in the mind of the drugged individual. For this reason, consumers of the drug often make the mistake of taking too much, thinking that nothing has happened, and re-administering the dose; however, in reality, the drug effect is so strong that they believe everything they see and cannot distinguish it in any way from reality. They may lose touch altogether with the real world, and become unable to converse with people or understand what is happening to them. Most individuals who have had this experience describe it as extremely unpleasant, frightening, and damaging to their sense of self, and sense of the world around them.

TRUTH OR SUPERSTITION?

The exact nature of the bokor's activities regarding the creation of zombies is shrouded in mystery, most of the stories being a product of folklore and superstition rather than rational research. However, according to the legend, after being revived by the bokor, the victim has no power of speech, no memory and no personality. Because of this, he or she is easy to control, and can be used by the bokor for a variety of tasks, including acting as a personal servant, or joining a labour force for agricultural or construction work.

There are various approaches to the zombie myth that attempt to tease out the truth about the idea of reanimating corpses. Some, including most Vodouisants, of course, believe that the bokor is capable of powerful magic, and is able to perform this task on a regular basis, so much so that many Haitians leading ordinary lives are thought by local people to be zombies. Less credulous sources take the line that the bokor does, in fact, use powerful drugs to induce coma-like states and hallucinations,

and may be able to subject a victim to a trance-like state over time. These accounts point to the medical effects of puffer-fish poison and *Datura*, and to apparent zombie sightings (see page 67). There are also those who believe that the entire zombie myth is simply a symbolic way of describing the turbulent political history of Haiti, especially the period of the Tontons Macoutes (see page 62), whose brutal behaviour was marked by an apparent disregard for human feeling, causing the population to believe that they must be zombies – victims of 'mind control' by the harsh dictatorship of the time.

THE PENAL CODE

Whatever the truth of the matter, fear of zombification by the bokor was enough, in Haiti, to warrant a law in the penal code of the country, specifying:

It shall also be qualified as attempted murder the employment, which may be made against any person, of substances which, without causing actual death, produce a lethargic coma more or less prolonged. If, after the person had been buried, the act shall be considered murder no matter what result follows.

Thus, whether or not puffer-fish or *Datura* poisoning actually led to death, the law of the land made it clear that inducing comas, hallucinations, or other such dabblings in the black arts of mind control were to be regarded as serious attempts on a person's life, and as such treated as criminal activities.

ZOMBIE POWDER

As with all aspects of zombie lore, the exact nature of zombie powder is highly mysterious. This legendary powder, used by the bokor in the creation of zombie slaves, is said to be highly toxic, including ingredients such as puffer-fish poison and *Datura stramonium* – the zombie's cucumber. In addition, there may be other ingredients added to the powder to increase its effect, such as crushed lizards, mystical herbs, hallucinogenic mushrooms and mixtures of blood, skin, hair and bones, all of which are believed by voodoo priests to have magical properties. Ground glass, which serves as an irritant, making the powder quicker to absorb, may also be added to the mixture.

In preparing the zombie powder, the bokor is thought to undergo certain rituals, which must, it is believed, be carefully observed in order for the potion to work. Individual bokors vary their rites and practices, but in general, they are said to make their preparations at night, in places 'where the dead are remembered'. Spirits are called up, prayers intoned, and magic spells cast. Should these sacred rites be interrupted for any reason, it is believed that the powder may cease to have an effect.

TRAPPED IN THEIR BODIES

There are few eye-witness accounts of the zombification procedure, but according to legend, the bokor applies the powder to the skin of the victim's face, taking care not to touch it himself. The powder takes effect almost immediately, being absorbed through breathing, through the eyes and through the mucous membranes of the lips and gums. As the powder enters the eye, it causes near blindness, which is the first symptom of the poisoning. In a few seconds, other disturbing symptoms occur: the victim will begin to breathe unevenly, lose his or her sense of balance and start to become delirious. Eventually, the victim will become paralysed and pass into the vegetative state that has been described as zombification.

Within twenty minutes of the administration of the zombie powder, the victim will be completely incapacitated. Four to six hours later, he or she will seem, to all intents and purposes, dead. The pulse will be so light, and the breathing so shallow, as to be undetectable except by special medical equipment. However, despite these alarming signs of death, the victims may actually still be conscious, and to some degree aware of what is happening to them. Nevertheless, they are unable to respond to any physical stimuli, because their bodies are completely paralysed. In this way, they are trapped in their bodies, unable to ask for help. To make matters worse for the victim, they may be undergoing bizarre, frightening hallucinations as a result of the *Datura*, and may not ever recover from the experience, permanently losing the ability to experience life in a normal way, which contributes to their zombified state.

SPIKING DRINKS

In certain circumstances, for example, when the bokor is unable to lure his victim to a place where the treatment can be administered, he may decide to use the powder to spike the victim's drink. This, apparently, is less successful, because the powder becomes diluted, making it difficult to predict the victim's reaction. Also, the victim may not consume the whole drink, so that the full amount may not be taken in, and instead of becoming paralysed, may only experience short-lived but intensely confusing and unpleasant sensations of reality distortion.

In some cases, the zombie powder will be used by the bokor to kill someone, rather than to create a willing slave. For the purposes of murder, the zombie powder is an effective way of rendering a victim comatose, so that they become defenceless, and it is easy to kill or bury them. In Haiti, gruesome stories abound of victims who wake up underground after burial, only to suffocate to death.

TRUTH OR LEGEND?

How much credibility these stories have is a matter of much conjecture among medical researchers, cultural historians, and anthropologists. Where it has been possible to analyse the contents of zombie powder, the results have varied: some research claims that the bokor's powder contains the elements described above, while others have found that it has no toxic properties whatsoever (see page 79). As with so much of zombie lore, it is difficult to establish the exact truth about this strange legend. However, we do know that the idea of zombification – that is, drugging individuals and using them to follow orders – has been well documented and occurs in many cultures.

THE BERSERKERS

Prior to the thirteenth century, we find tales of old Norse warriors who were known as *berserkers* because they went into battle in a trance-like state, becoming savage and uncontrollable, like wild animals. Their behaviour was described thus:

This fury, which was called berserkergang, *occurred not only in the heat of battle, but also during laborious work. Men who were thus seized performed things which otherwise seemed impossible for human power. This condition is said to have begun with shivering, chattering of the teeth, and chill in the body, and then the face swelled and changed its colour. With this was connected a great hot-headedness, which at last gave over into a great rage, under which they howled as wild animals, bit the edge of their shields, and cut down everything they met without discriminating between friend or foe. When this condition ceased, a great dulling of the mind and feebleness followed, which could last for one or several days.*

Historians now believe that the Norse berserkers may have been given hallucinogenic herbs and medicines before battle, making them more or less insane; insensible to any danger to themselves, and also extremely violent.

THE HASHSHASHIN

In the same way, there are medieval tales of Arabic fighters called the *hashshashin*, a group of fierce Muslim fighters, from whom the word assassin originates. The exact derivation of the name is unclear: it may have simply meant 'followers of Hassan', but for many years it was taken to mean 'hashish users', or, alternatively, 'people addled as if by hashish'. In the thirteenth century, the explorer Marco Polo described a visit to the East in which he told of assassins who were drugged as part of an initiation rite to simulate dying. When they awoke, they found themselves in a dream, and were served a delicious feast of wine and food by beautiful virgins. Convinced they were in heaven, the soldiers saw their leader appear as a god, commanding them to fight to the death in the battles they undertook, and to follow his orders under all

circumstances. After the drugging episode, the hashshashin would be effectively brainwashed, and would go on to commit hideous atrocities in war, showing no signs of mercy to their victims.

The truth of such tales has since been questioned. In all these stories, whether concerning the zombies, the beserkers, or the hashshashin, even if we believe in the process of drugging and brainwashing, it is difficult to understand how drugged individuals, whether forced into hard labour or violent conflict, would be able to function properly in a comatose, or semi-comatose state. But whatever the truth, there is no doubt that these legends have persisted, over the centuries, in many different cultures, and continue to do so today.

It may be the case that, where human beings show inhuman characteristics, such as the ability to behave like a 'zombie', ruthlessly following orders, however cruel they may be, we tend to seek explanations for their acting in terms of drugs, and inculcation. According to this point of view, the Haitian zombie myth is an attempt to explain how an entire population could have been subjugated, completely losing their free will in the process. In the same way, medieval people may also have attempted to explain the brutal behaviour of the berserkers and hashshashin, pointing to drugging and brainwashing as a way of stripping them of their humanity.

CHARACTERISTICS OF THE HAITIAN ZOMBIE

In Haitian folklore, zombies created by the bokor are more or less harmless. In contrast to the Hollywood zombie, who is a rapacious monster, the Haitian zombie is characterised as a humble, broken, and rather weak being with little or no willpower. Haitian zombies have, according to the legend, lost their souls, which have been captured by the bokor. For this reason, they lead empty lives, devoid of the will to harm others or, indeed, to experience any emotions at all. Their task is simply to serve the bokor as slaves, regardless of their own desires.

The Haitians view the fate of the zombie as a miserable one, but on the whole the zombie is not seen as aggressive. However, if commanded by their masters to kill, maim or destroy, zombies will follow orders and commit any crime, however bloodthirsty. Since they have no emotional life, they are incapable of remorse or pity, which makes them brutal and dangerous opponents.

One of the characteristics of the zombie is that he or she is incapable of remembering the past, thus severing all ties with family, friends and their homes. Zombies have no affection for anyone or anything, and are unable to recognise former loved ones. It is impossible for any human being to form a relationship of any kind with a zombie, whether of love, friendship or even animosity. However, in certain situations,

zombies may show a glimmer of their former selves – for example, when confronted with an intense emotional situation, such as the death of a family member in their previous life – but this is rare. To all intents and purposes, the zombie is an undead being who has lost its humanity, becoming a machine – a body – used only for the purposes of hard labour and servitude.

Unlike the lurid depictions of the zombie in the movies, which show these creatures covered in rotting flesh, slavering for blood, the Haitian zombie looks exactly like any 'normal' person, and shows no lustful instincts whatsoever. This is because zombies have no feelings at all, whether of love, hatred or the desire to destroy. It is precisely this quality, of seeming ordinary on the outside, but being inwardly dead –

truly, the 'walking dead' – that horrified the Haitian peasants, and struck fear into their hearts.

This version of the zombie, as visually conventional but emotionally inhuman has many links with other myths concerning supernatural beings, such as the vampire myth and the werewolf myth. In all these cases, there is a tension between the 'normal' aspect of the being and the 'deviant', giving rise to many stories that express the conflict between these two split personalities, and the way that human beings are both fascinated and repelled by signs of otherness in those around them.

THE EYES OF A DEAD MAN

In 1929, William B. Seabrook published an extraordinary account of his experiences in Haiti, entitled, *The Magic Island*. This seminal book introduced the Western world to the idea of the zombie. In it, he described how a section of the Vodou religion practised on the island dedicated itself to the world of the dead, much to the disgust, he emphasised, of many conventional Vodouisants, who wanted nothing to do with it. He recounted how the bokors created the zombie, and told of meeting one of these creatures on his travels, whom he characterised as a humble field worker, rather than the slavering monster of the Hollywood B movie genre:

The eyes were the worst. It was not my imagination. They were in truth like the eyes of a dead man, not blind, but staring, unfocussed, unseeing. The whole face, for that matter, was bad enough. It was vacant, as if there was nothing behind it. It seemed not only expressionless, but incapable of expression.

WITH THESE ZOMBIE EYES
he rendered her powerless

WHITE ZOMBIE

WITH THIS ZOMBIE GRIP
he made her perform his every desire

Seabrook's book caused a stir, and the image of the zombie soon found its way into the burgeoning film industry of the time, in a movie called *White Zombie*, made in 1932 (see page 100). Here, we find zombies much as Seabrook had described them: ordinary labourers toiling in the cane fields of Haiti, with the vacant, staring eyes of those suffering extreme poverty and hardship. In the film, the zombies have been created for one purpose, and one purpose only: to work. This is akin to the chains of slavery Haiti had faced over the past couple of centuries. Later, of course, the image of the zombie became more lurid – a decomposing corpse with an insatiable hunger for human flesh – but in this groundbreaking film, the Vodou idea of zombies as mindless, 'undead' human beings with no capacity for emotion, created for, and condemned to, a life of hard labour was deemed disturbing enough.

MIND-DEAD SLAVES

It is no accident that this notion of the zombie as a mind-dead slave should have originated in Haiti, where successive conflicts and brutal exploitation had reduced almost the entire population of the country to grinding poverty . What was clearly being described in the tale of the zombie was a situation in which ordinary workers, ground down by poverty and hard labour, with no hope for the future, were in danger of losing their souls and their will to live. The myth of the zombie was a metaphor; expressing the Haitians' fear that the terrible hardship of their lives might end up

robbing them of their humanity, and indeed, anyone who has seen people starving, living in extreme poverty, or condemned to a life of hard labour, barely scratching a living, will recognise Seabrook's description of the vacant eyes and expressionless face of the 'zombie', the human being forced to live like an animal, with no hope for the future, and no possibility of changing their situation.

The zombie legend is also intimately connected to the idea of capitalism and industrialisation. As the zombie master Legendre comments in *White Zombie*, discussing his army of slaves, 'They work faithfully and are not worried about long hours.' In Haitian Vodou, great emphasis is placed on the 'mind control' effected by the bokor over his slave, which mimics the way that the capitalist attempts to control the worker, reducing his or her ability to make choices, assert any kind of individuality, or express free will. In this way, the legend of the zombie can be seen as a critique of capitalism, pointing out the way in which the ordinary individual is exploited, becoming a cog in a machine, and in the process losing his or her humanity.

ZOMBIES AND MENTAL ILLNESS

Some commentators believe that the idea of the zombie may have been used to explain the symptoms of a person suffering from mental illness. In extreme forms of illnesses such as schizophrenia, individuals may enter a catatonic phase, experiencing a loss of consciousness or trance-like state. They may become unable to converse, and seem to lose most of the signs of cognition. They may also lose all desire to eat, drink, move around and engage with other people. In severe cases, they may adopt particular positions and hold them, so that their limbs have to be moved around by their carers. In addition, they may lose their memory, and fail to recognise loved ones. It is not hard to see why peasant folk, with no knowledge of science and no access to medical help, viewed such mental states, as zombification and the malign curse of the bokor, rather than an illness.

The Scottish psychiatrist R. D. Laing also made a further link between mental illness and capitalism. According to his argument, schizophrenia may, in some individuals, be a reaction to repressive social rules and expectations. Forcing imaginative, eccentric, or idiosyncratic people into a strictly controlled social order, may sometimes, he argued, spark off schizophrenia and other mental illnesses. His view was that, in general, capitalist society is ordered in such a way as to threaten the mental health of its members, since so little opportunity is given for people to engage in individual expression, assert their freedom of will, or adopt ways of life that contradict the norms of the modern, industrialised world.

Nowhere could this be more true than in Haiti, where even today, the majority of the population

are forced into agricultural labour, suffering intense hardship, poverty and deprivation. In this way, some argue, the people of Haiti have been 'zombified' by a succession of leaders, both Western capitalists and corrupt dictators, whose sole aim has been to exploit their land and labour, enslaving the citizens to feed their own greed, and depriving them almost entirely of their freedom. No wonder that such a country would express this history in a folklore, culture and religion that tells the story of the dehumanised zombie as the slave of the evil bokor, who has stolen his soul.

ZOMBIE MAGIC

Outsiders may regard the zombie lore of Haiti as no more than superstition, but on the island it exerts a powerful force. To this day the bokor, or sorceror, is a prestigious individual, widely respected and feared for his arcane ability to perform the reanimation of the dead in the ceremony known as the *deadsender*. There are many rumours concerning this ritual, but it is thought that the bokor goes to the graveyard at midnight to commune with Baron Samedi, the lwa who commands the dead.

BARON SAMEDI

Baron Samedi is a member of the *Guede* family of lwa, or spirits, who rules over death and fertility with his wife, Maman Brigitte. Pictures of him often show a skeleton dressed in a white top hat, suit, and dark glasses, carrying a can with a skull carved into it. His nose is plugged with cotton wool, in the same way that a corpse is prepared for the coffin. His character is debauched, and although he is married to another powerful lwa, he is a seducer of mortal humans, both men and women and is sometimes represented by a phallic symbol. He drinks rum and smokes tobacco, uses foul language, tells dirty jokes and likes to disrupt polite ceremonies. Baron Samedi controls the world of the dead, and must be approached each time there is a new candidate for the graveyard, since it is he who protects those within its walls.

However, as well as ruling the dead, he also has the power to reanimate, and is able to restore life, even when someone has been mortally wounded. In addition, when someone is near to death, especially because of a curse, he may refuse to dig their grave, in which case they will be restored back to health.

Another of the Baron's tasks is to make sure his community of corpses in the graveyard stay dead. He ensures that their bodies rot away in peace, and is particularly careful to ensure that no one is stolen away by the bokor to be made into a zombie slave.

To keep Baron Samedi happy, he must be given regular gifts of rum, cigars, black coffee, peanuts and bread. His followers are required to wear black, purple or white, and use certain sacred objects in worshipping him. If he is required to make a visit to the human world, the right prayers and incantations must be said, and sacrifices of animals offered.

she guards the graveyard, and will protect graves marked with a cross

MAMAN BRIGITTE

The Baron consorts with a host of other badly-behaved spirits, including his wife Maman Brigitte, who is sometimes represented by a black cockerel. Like her husband, she guards the graveyard, and will protect graves marked with a cross. However, she must be offered incentives to do so. She has a particular liking for a red hot chilli pepper drink laced with hot rum. People claiming to be possessed by her must drink this rum, or have red peppers rubbed into their genitals. It is thought that if this process is painful to them, they are lying.

Some cultural historians trace Mama Brigitte's roots to the Irish pagan goddess Brigid. They believe that this saint, who was highly regarded as a mistress of the druidic arts, was brought to the Americas by early Irish immigrants who intermarried with African slaves. Through this mingling of peoples and cultures, it is thought that within Haitian voodoo, some elements of Celtic paganism survive. Indeed, with their irrepressible pantheon of mercurial gods and goddesses, and their belief that natural objects have spirits attached to them, the Celts' world view appears to have had much in common with African Vodun, and seems to have been an influence in the creation of Haitian voodoo.

TRICKING THE LORD OF THE DEAD

As we have seen, in some cases the bokor creates zombies by rubbing a paralysing magic powder onto his victims, sending them into a deep coma before reanimating them as mindless slaves. However, in other cases, where there maybe a short-supply of live victims, the bokor must visit the graveyard to find a dead body, and try to bring it back to life through the same process.

In order to do this, the bokor must trick Baron Samedi, the protector of the dead, into letting one of his residents be taken away from the cemetery. According to legend, the bokor creeps to the grave of the body he has his eye on, and in front of the headstone, evokes a powerful demon. If the bokor is successful in this endeavour, the demon will help him – catching the dead body's spirit and keeping it safe in a bottle. The bokor will then invoke a spell to put Baron Samedi to sleep, and while he is sleeping, dig up the corpse. He will reanimate the corpse with more spells, and lead it out of the graveyard as a zombie. Without its own spirit, the zombie will have no will of its own, and will become a slave to the bokor for eternity.

'A MECHANICAL APPEARANCE OF LIFE'

In his book published in 1929, *The Magic Island*, the American occultist and explorer, William Seabrook, described how, at the time of his visit to Haiti, belief in zombie magic was still a central part of the local population's spiritual life. He described how he heard rumours among the people of an undead, ghostly being in the form of a body without a soul: that is, a person who is 'clinically dead, but magically regains a purely mechanical appearance of life; a corpse that acts, moves, walks as if it was alive, thanks to the crafts of a wizard.'

According to these rumours, which Seabrook went on to detail, the wizard chooses a recently buried corpse that has not begun to decompose, then somehow galvanises it into life. Having created this mechanical beast, the wizard then enslaves it, ordering it to commit heinous crimes, which it will execute without pity. He may also order the zombie to work hard, day and night, performing heavy agricultural labour or endless domestic tasks. In this way, the zombie is condemned to a life of forced labour, without even the promise of death to relieve its burden.

THE CASE OF TI JOSEPH

Seabrook was surprised to find that educated people on the island, as well as the local peasant population, also believed these rumours. According to his Haitian friend, an ordinarily quite sceptical man named Costantino Polinice, the practice of creating zombies was a well documented one on the island, and not a matter of mere superstition.

Polinice told him of an elderly black man named Ti-Joseph du Columbier, who had been seen one day arriving at the fields followed by a group of ragged labourers. These labourers all had a drugged expression, and walked with a shuffling pace. They appeared to be under a spell, and did whatever the old man told them, without speaking a word, showing a passive obedience to him that was extremely unusual in young, strong men taking orders from a frail old man.

Ti-Joseph set his men to work in the fields under the beating sun, where they continued to labour for hours on end without a break. They sought no shade, rarely stopped to eat or drink, and never spoke a word, either to each other or to passers by. They were out in the fields for days, during which time they slept very little, and ate only bananas.

BREAKING THE SPELL

One day, when Ti-Joseph was absent, a Haitian woman chanced to pass by. She was selling salted pistachio nuts, and out of kindness offered the men some. When they tasted the salt they suddenly realised they were in fact reanimated corpses and ran back to their tombs in the graveyard. Each of them found their own grave, and began to dig, desperate to get back under the ground. When they finally managed to do so, and laid themselves in their graves, their bodies immediately began to rot, and had to be hastily covered with soil before they decomposed altogether.

Polinice explained that, according to Haitian legend, zombies must never be given meat to eat or salt on

zombies must never be given meat to eat or salt on their food

their food. If this happens, they will break the spell that keeps them alive, realize their enslaved condition, and run to their graves as quickly as they can.

BEASTS OF BURDEN

In addition to this strange story, Seabrook added his own observations. In one instance, he told how he and his friend Polinicc travelled around the island and saw a group of labourers digging the earth on a mountainside. The four of them, three men and a woman, worked without stopping, 'like beasts, like automatons'. When Seabrook and Polinice approached them, they showed no curiosity, but looked at them without expression, their faces blank, and then returned to their labours.

Although Seabrook later convinced himself that the workers must have been mentally subnormal, he continued to feel uneasy about what he had seen. When he mentioned the episode to another friend, a doctor named Antoine Villiers, whom he described as having a 'pragmatic scientific mind', the doctor said he believed that there was some kind of 'horrible witchcraft' being practised on the island, and that the stories had some basis in truth. The doctor also showed him an article from the Haitian penal code (see page 41), outlawing this kind of criminal activity, which suggested the practice of drugging individuals, inducing comas for long periods of time, and burying live human beings, did indeed take place on the island, and were a serious threat to the security of the population.

THE ZOMBIE MYTH

To understand the power of the zombie myth in Haiti, we must look at the country's varied cultural make-up and its extraordinary history as the first and only country in the world to gain independence as the result of a slave rebellion. However, today it remains the poorest country in the Americas, with a population that has suffered greatly over the years from a combination of war, poverty, corruption and a series of terrible natural disasters.

'A MOUNTAINOUS LAND'

Haiti occupies the western part of the island of Hispaniola. The other section is occupied by the Dominican Republic. Originally, the island was inhabited by the Taino, who were sailors from the Arawak tribe in South America. The Taino Arawaks named their land Ayiti, meaning 'mountainous land'. In those early days, it was a rich, lush island: sixty per cent of its mountains and valleys were covered in forest. (Today, only two per cent of the forests remain, causing persistent problems of flooding and landslides.) Its people also called it 'Boho', meaning 'rich villages' and 'Kiskeya', meaning 'the cradle of life'. This paradise, however, came to an abrupt end with the arrival of Christopher Columbus, who landed there on 5 December 1492, claiming it for the Spanish crown. As history records, the indigenous Taino people, including Queen Anacaona, their leader, tried to resist. However, to no avail. They were defeated by the invaders, and the Queen was captured and publicly executed. Today, Queen Anacaona is revered in Haiti as one of the founders of the nation.

'ZOMBIE SLAVES'

The Spanish conquistadors then went on to establish settlements all over the island, creating a tyrannical regime. They systematically robbed the country of its natural resources, exporting its gold, and forcing the native people to work in their mines. In this way, the first 'real zombies', indigenous Taino slaves working like robots for their colonial masters, were born.

Any native people who refused to comply with their new Spanish rulers were summarily executed or enslaved for life. In addition to these miseries, the Spanish also brought numerous diseases with them, including smallpox, which decimated the indigenous population. Only a very small number of Taino survivors escaped to the hills, where they went on to form outlaw settlements.

AFRICAN DIASPORA

In the years that followed, the Spanish found another source of 'real zombies' to work in the mines and fields of Hispaniola: slaves imported from Africa. These people were imported to the island in great numbers, swelling the ranks of the indigenous workers already toiling in the mines and fields. Some of these newly immigrated African slaves went on the run and encountered the Taino in the hills. The African maroons, as the runaway slaves were called, mixed with the Taino, producing a generation of African/Amerindian children known as 'zambos'. In addition to the Taino/

African mixed-race offspring, many African slave women bore children to their European masters, often as a result of rape. These African/European children were called 'mulattos'. Thus, from these early times, there was an extraordinary mixing of ethnic backgrounds and cultures among the people of Haiti, forming a new culture with its roots in a variety of spiritual belief systems from across the world.

French buccaneers also arrived on the island, adding their culture and beliefs to the mix. These adventurers eventually settled in Haiti as farmers, growing tobacco for an increasing market, and reaping rich rewards in the process, much to the consternation of the Spanish, with whom the newcomers fought many battles.

THE BLACK CODE

While the French and Spanish colonists fought over the island, the local population of slaves continued to labour in the plantations, producing sugar, coffee and indigo. Within a few short years, the island became a brutal slave colony, a hive of workers living in dire poverty and making immense profits for their masters. Meanwhile, the French rulers, who had gained the upper hand in parts of the island, enacted the Black Code, a set of rules laying down the most hideously barbaric conditions for the slaves. Thus, the slaves – the 'real zombies' of Haitian history – were deprived of their freedom, their humanity and in many cases, their lives. Around a third of slaves imported from Africa died shortly after arrival, and those who went on to survive lived like animals until they died.

In this context, one can imagine why the idea of reanimation – being brought back from the dead – might be thought of as the slave's worst nightmare. To the labouring masses on the island, death must have seemed, in many cases, like a blessed relief from a life of toil, poverty, disease and general misery. The zombie legend, in which the corpse of a recently deceased individual is brought back and enslaved by the bokor, pinpointed the slaves' fear that their desperate grind might be eternal, and might never cease, even in death.

'ZOMBIE' REVOLT

In the wake of the French Revolution (1789–1799), the former slave Toussaint L'Ouverture mounted a massive revolt against the colonists, leading his rebel band to victory. He then managed the amazing feat of establishing peace and prosperity on the island, driving out the rapacious entrepreneurs and insisting that labourers work on the plantations as freed men and women. However, it was not long before the ousted colonists fought back.

In 1801 Napoleon Bonaparte sent a force to retake the island, and through a mixture of trickery, cunning and deceit, the colonists captured L'Ouverture. He was taken from the island and imprisoned in France, where he died of illness in 1803, a broken man. However, his ally, Jean-Jacques Dessalines, went on to defeat the French troops, freed the slaves once again, and in 1804 proclaimed the new nation as Haiti, using the ancient Taino name.

PERMANENT CONFLICT

Sadly, Dessalines proved to be a despotic leader, and was assassinated two years later. France once again tried to retake the island, this time demanding a huge sum of money as an indemnity for profits lost from the slave trade. The country slid into anarchy and a state of almost permanent conflict, as coups and revolts against successive governments took place. There was much bloodshed, and the gains that were made for the people were rolled back until once more, they were living in poverty. Thus it was that the first – and last – successful slave revolt in the Americas came to an ignominious end.

THE DUVALIER DYNASTY

In 1956 François Duvalier, known informally to his people as 'Papa Doc' was elected President of Haiti. In one of the most catastrophic episodes in Haiti's turbulent history, this so-called 'man of the people', who emphasised his image as an indigenous black Haitian, went on to declare himself President-for-Life and became one of the worst tyrants of modern times.

THE 'REAL' BARON SAMEDI

François 'Papa Doc' Duvalier was born in Port-au-Prince, the son of a justice of the peace and Ulyssia Abraham. Ulyssia had a history of mental illness and was confined for many years in a mental asylum. As it transpired, this trait was to have a bearing on her son's mental condition, but this did not emerge until many years later.

THE STUDY OF VODOU

On completing his university medical training, the young François embarked on valuable work in the treatment of tropical diseases on the island. He also became interested in the concept of 'black pride' and began to study the native Vodou culture of Haiti. During these years, through his careful study, he gained knowledge that would later be immensely valuable to him in persuading the superstitious indigenous population of poor Haitians to follow him.

After serving as a minister, and waiting out a series of coups, Duvalier ran for president, gaining the office in 1956. There was much rejoicing that at last a black leader had come to power in Haiti, but as soon as the new president took control, it became clear that the Haitian people had made a major error of judgement.

Duvalier was unable to tolerate opposition of any kind, and exiled or imprisoned all those who spoke out against his totalitarian regime. He created a personality cult around himself, and soon began to show disturbing signs of insanity. Styling himself on the sinister spirit, Baron Samedi, he began to wear sunglasses and talk in a high, nasal tone. (These were characteristics of the Baron in popular lore.) Papa Doc cleverly manipulated the uneducated, superstitious people of the country, claiming that he was a Houngan or Vodou priest, that he consorted with the loa or spirits, and that, moreover, Jesus Christ had personally endorsed his presidency. A poster at the time showed Duvalier sitting with the hand of Christ on his shoulder, and the caption, 'I have chosen him'.

THE TONTON MACOUTES: 'REAL' ZOMBIES

Vodou mythology came to play a central part in Haitian politics. Duvalier used it to bolster his position, appealing to the superstitious beliefs of the native population to ensure his popularity. Not only this, he instituted a reign of terror on the island, establishing a rural militia, the Milice Volontaires de la Sécurité Nationale, better known as the Tonton Macoutes.

The name Tonton Macoute comes from Haitian mythology. 'Uncle Gunnysack' or 'Tonton Macoute' is a bogeyman who prowls around after dark, looking for children to put in his sack. According to this folk tale, when the children are kidnapped, they are never seen again. Mothers in Haiti often threatened their children that unless they came home before dark, the Tonton Macoute would get them.

Duvalier's new paramilitary force soon got this nickname, and it turned out to be well deserved. His men would call on people in the night, take them away, and their family and friends would never see them again. Sometimes they were killed, sometimes imprisoned; but their whereabouts, in most cases, were never revealed. Those who met this terrifying fate were almost always opponents of the regime, especially those who had questioned Duvalier's wisdom or proposed reforms.

In addition, the soldiers sent for the victims gained a reputation as vicious, brutal and bloodthirsty. Like zombie slaves, they did their master's bidding, showing no mercy, even to people they knew, such as former family, friends and neighbours. Thus the suspicion arose that Duvalier had put his henchmen under a spell, causing them to become a kind of 'walking dead', loyal to him under all circumstances. The fact that the Tonton Macoutes were also open to corruption, and often practised extortion for personal gain, did little to dispel this fear.

DECAPITATED HEAD

In 1959, Duvalier became ill and suffered a heart attack which left him unconscious for nine hours. After his recovery, his mental health appeared to deteriorate further, and he became extremely paranoid and as superstitious as those he ruled over. He imprisoned the leader of the Tonton Macoutes, Clement Barbot, suspecting him of plotting against him and trying to oust him from the presidency. After this, the Tonton Macoutes went on to become even more violent, murdering, torturing and terrorising thousands of innocent victims during Duvalier's rule while continuing to show a craven loyalty to their tyrannical leader.

THE DEATH OF PAPA DOC

In 1964, after another bogus election, Duvalier proclaimed himself President-for-Life.The human rights atrocities in Haiti continued, and many educated, skilled people fled in terror from the island, creating further problems for this already desperately poor and troubled land.

According to some estimates, Duvalier was responsible for murdering over 30,000 of his opponents during his reign of terror. Like a medieval monarch, he also tried to secure rule for his descendents: on his death in 1971, the mantle of the presidency was passed, without democratic elections, to his nineteen-year-old son Jean-Claude, who was immediately dubbed 'Baby Doc'.

BABY DOC

Under the new president, Baby Doc, the situation in Haiti grew even worse. The young president continued to live as a playboy, leaving most of the affairs of state to his mother. His corrupt regime funded his luxurious lifestyle, stealing from the public purse in a way that had by now become quite normal among the higher echelons of the Haitian administration.

OBSCENE EXTRAVAGANCE

The new president was lucky enough to be tolerated by the people of Haiti for a while, until he made a major error. He married an extremely unpopular woman, a mixed-race or mulatto divorcee named Michele Bennett Pasquet. Her first husband, also a mulatto, had attempted a coup to overthrow Papa Doc. In addition, Michele Bennett's father, Ernest, was a businessman whose shady dealings included selling Haitian cadavers to foreign medical schools – another bizarre link to the zombie myth on the island.

While Papa Doc had been feared and hated by many in Haiti, he had managed to retain power by allying himself with the black majority, emphasising the African cultural heritage of voodoo and showing considerable antipathy to the light-skinned elite who had held power in former times. Baby Doc, by marrying into this elite, broke the final bond with the people. Moreover, the obscene extravagance of the couple's wedding, which was reported to have cost over three million US dollars, made them even more unpopular, and the scene was set for the fall of the Duvalier dynasty.

DRUG DEALER

Once Baby Doc had married his new wife, her father Ernest Bennett began to use the connection to further his business interests, amassing enormous wealth in a very short space of time. As well as having a reputation for corruption, Bennett was also rumoured to be a drug dealer, using his airline to make deliveries. Meanwhile, the new first lady, Michele Duvalier, became known for her cruel behaviour and her addiction to shopping. The couple lived in opulent luxury at their home, the National Palace, and threw huge parties there. In one instance, Baby Doc dressed as a sultan, and handed out hugely expensive jewels worth over US$10,000 each to guests. He thoughtfully supplied the homeless population with televisions in the parks so that they could watch the extravagant festivities.

'SOMETHING MUST CHANGE'

Not surprisingly, there was considerable unrest among the people, whose living standards were deteriorating further while the Duvaliers flaunted their wealth. When the Pope visited the island in 1983, he was moved to declare that 'something must change' in Haiti, which added fuel to the fire. There were popular protests against the regime within Haiti, and mounting opposition to it internationally. Duvalier responded by clamping down further on security, and by cutting the price of staple foods on the island; but it was only a matter of time before revolt rose up.

Duvalier, whose regime had become a byword for brutality and corruption, tried to cling to power, but eventually he and his family were forced to flee. Many countries denied them asylum, but they were allowed to settle in France. When authorities finally investigated looting allegations against them, Michele Duvalier was found to have spent enormous sums of money on jewellery, clothes and luxury hotels.

The couple later divorced, but both continue to live in exile in Paris.

A LIVING HELL

However, Haiti's troubles were far from over. In 1987, general elections were disrupted by the notorious Tonton Macoutes, who shot dozens of people, both in the cities and the rural areas. A new government, led by Jean-Bertrand Aristide, came into power in 1991, but within months, he was ousted in a coup d'état, and had to flee into exile. With the help of the US government, his presidency was restored, only to fall again as a result of allegations of corruption. Aristide was succeeded, after an interim period, by Rene Preval, who is the current president of Haiti.

In addition to these political upheavals, Haiti has the highest levels of HIV/Aids outside Africa. Efforts at prevention and treatment are hamstrung by fear, superstition – many believe the disease to be treatable only by voodoo priests – and the armed gangs that rule the city slums.

In addition the island is renowned for experiencing terrible tropical weather conditions. A string of hurricanes and tropical storms in recent years coupled with deforestation causing constant landslides and flooding. The devastating earthquake of January 2010 flattened the capital Port-au-Prince, causing 200,000 deaths.

A NATION OF 'REAL' ZOMBIES?

Bearing in mind this turbulent history, it may seem that the poverty-stricken people of Haiti, over the centuries, have at times been condemned to a living hell. No wonder that their religion and culture is full of such dark images as undead zombies and corrupt figures like the bokor and Baron Samedi. For many Haitians, being forced to work like automatons without human souls, serving greedy, cruel masters who have no respect for them as human beings, has been the reality of their lives. Thus it is that the legend of the zombie slave serving a heartless master is not just a mythical tale from the island's folklore; it is also metaphor for the painful history of the Haitian people over centuries of exploitation and misrule, not only by the colonists but by their own elected representatives.

It is fascinating to trace, in the island's troubled past, how the Vodun religion, and voodoo generally, has played such an important role there. In particular, the figure of Papa Doc seems to raise many contradictions. Although towards the end of his rule he was almost universally reviled, he seemed to be able to continue his despotic rule for many years by emulating the coarse behaviour of the loa spirit Baron Samedi. Obviously, much of his support was due to the fact that he was a black man, steeped in the culture of the country, whereas most of Haiti's rulers had been from a mixed-race or European ethnic background. But this does not entirely explain his appeal.

VICIOUS INSANITY

It may simply be that, having instituted a reign of terror with the Tonton Macoutes over the years,

Duvalier was able to quell any sign of opposition, so that the people's estimation of him as leader was no longer an issue.

VOODOO AND POLITICS

Whatever the case, there is no doubt that voodoo, with its legend of the zombie slave and the bokor, has played a major part in Haitian politics. By tapping into the mythology of voodoo, Papa Doc managed to retain control over the island for decades. Significantly, his son was less successful. Where perhaps the people of Haiti were prepared to tolerate the sins of Papa Doc, respecting him to some extent as voodoo priest or as the divine modern incarnation of the uncouth loa Baron Samedi, they drew the line at showing the same devotion to Baby Doc, a spoilt playboy who who appeared simply to step into his father's shoes, reducing them once more to the status of a nation of 'real' zombies working for an evil, corrupt master.

ZOMBIE SIGHTINGS

Today, most believe the zombies of Haitian folklore to be creatures of legend, created by storytellers to explain the island's history of slavery in a metaphorical way. However, there have been several eminent folklorists, anthropologists and botanists who have argued that zombies on the island are a real phenomenon, and have presented evidence for their findings.

WILLIAM BUEHLER SEABROOK

The writer and explorer William Buehler Seabrook, published *The Magic Island* in 1929, detailing his travels on Haiti. Seabrook was an American from Westminster, Maryland, who started his career writing for the *Augusta Chronicle* in Georgia. After serving in the French army during World War One, during which time he was almost gassed to death, he went back to journalism, becoming a travelling reporter for the *New York Times*, and contributing to a number of other newspapers and magazines. Over the years that followed, he started to travel more and more widely, bringing back fascinating reports of life in distant countries for a sensation-hungry public. In the process, he began to take a more than passing interest in the occult, adopting some curious and rather unsavoury practices himself.

CANNIBAL TALES

One of the most bizarre stories that Seabrook filed was an account of a sojourn in West Africa among the cannibal Gucre tribe. One evening, he joined the tribe members in a meal of human meat, accompanied by rice. The meat was from a man who had recently died but had not been murdered, and had been prepared in several different ways. Seabrook described it thus: 'It was so nearly like good, fully developed veal that I think no person with a palate of ordinary, normal sensitiveness could distinguish it from veal. It was mild, good meat with no other sharply defined or highly characteristic taste such as for instance, goat, high game, and pork have. The steak was slightly tougher than prime veal, a little stringy, but not too tough or stringy to be agreeably edible. The roast, from which I cut and ate a central slice, was tender, and in color, texture, smell as well as taste, strengthened my certainty that of all

Above: Image from William Buehler Seabrook's *The Magic Island*, 1929.

the meats we habitually know, veal is the one meat to which this meat is accurately comparable.'

After detailing other aspects of life with the cannibals, Seabrook then went on to travel in Arabia, describing his encounters with 'Bedouins, Druses, Whirling Dervishes and Yezisee Devil Worshipers' in a book called *Adventures in Arabia*, published in 1927. His next stop was Haiti, where he found out about voodoo, in particular investigating stories of zombie slaves. His book, *The Magic Island*, detailed accounts of zombie sightings, told to him by friends and acquaintances, and also gave some first-hand experiences of seeing what he took to be zombie labourers on the island. However, although he was fascinated by the occult, he continued to believe that all such phenomena could be explained by recourse to science, expounding this theory in a book called *Witchcraft: Its Power in the World Today*, published in 1940.

SEABROOK'S ZOMBIE TALES

Seabrook holds the distinction of introducing the modern concept of the zombie to the western world, but he was by no means the author of the term. It is thought that the word *zombie*, in former times, was used in various Caribbean and South American countries to refer to a buried corpse that had been unearthed for some natural reason., such as flooding or landslides. However, Seabrook used *zombie* to mean a person raised from the dead, that is, a corpse brought back to life from the grave. In addition, Seabrook

presented this concept in a highly sensationalised way, describing the fixed, glazed look of the zombies he encountered on the island, who were all slaves or poverty-stricken labourers, and who might well have shown these traits through sheer exhaustion. It is no coincidence that, shortly after the publication of *The Magic Island*, the first zombie movie, *White Zombie*, starring Bela Lugosi, appeared on the screen (see page 100).

THE 'WALKING DEAD'

One of the most memorable features of *The Magic Island* was the illustrations of zombies by an artist called Alexander King. These images of the zombies, or 'walking dead', were the first to be seen in America, and were extremely striking. King later became a playwright and TV personality, but like Seabrook, his life was marked by addiction, illness, and marital problems. As a result of Seabrook's lurid tales, memorably illustrated by King, the zombie quickly joined the mummy, the vampire and the werewolf as stock-in-trades of the horror genre. However, the zombie remains unique as a figure with its origins in the shameful world of colonial labour. In *The Magic Island*, Seabrook alleged that zombies were reanimated so that they could work in the factories and cane fields on the island owned by the Haitian-American Sugar Company and other multinational corporations.

ALCOHOLISM AND SUICIDE

Sadly, William Seabrook's life ended in tragedy. For some years, he was resident in a mental hospital, suffering from alcoholism. In true investigative style, he published an account of the experience, *Asylum*, which became a bestseller. (He did not reveal that the patient in the account was himself, but wrote it as though he were an impartial observer.) Later in life, his marriage to novelist Marjorie Muir Worthington ended in divorce, and in 1945 he committed suicide by taking a drug overdose.

THE CASE OF FELICIA FELIX-MENTOR

During the late 1920s and early 1930s, when the Haitian zombie myth was beginning to come to the attention of the American public, a case of an alleged zombie sighting hit the headlines. In 1907 Felicia Felix-Mentor suddenly became ill, died, and was buried. However, in 1936, she reappeared. Half naked, clothed only in rags, she was dazed and confused. She told everyone, 'I used to live here.'

RAISED FROM THE DEAD?

Frightened by this strange apparition, the tenants tried to chase the woman off their land. However, when the owner of the farm arrived, he confirmed that the woman was a former family member, Felicia Felix-Mentor. He said that the woman was his sister, and she had died and been buried nearly thirty years previously.

The woman was taken to hospital and examined. Her husband was called in to see her, but was not keen to come, since he had no wish to disrupt the new life he had made for himself since her death. Eventually, the authorities forced him to pay a visit to the hospital and identify her, which he duly did, pronouncing that the woman was indeed his former wife.

There were numerous theories as to the true story that lay behind the re-appearance of Felicia Felix-Mentor. Some believed that the woman had been raised from the dead by a bokor or sorceror. Others were scornful, saying that she was merely a poor, confused woman wandering about the countryside, who happened to slightly resemble the original Felicia Felix-Mentor. Whatever the truth of the matter, the reporting of this incident did much to fan the flames of 'zombie panic' that took hold of certain communities, both in and outside of Haiti, at this time.

LOUIS P. MARS

In 1945, a Haitian professor of psychiatry named Louis P. Mars published a paper in a learned journal, *Man: A Record of Anthropological Science*. This was entitled *The Story of the Zombi in Haiti*, and in it, Mars tried to give a scientific account of this particular case. He began by explaining that, in certain rural areas of Haiti, there is a belief that rich peasants are helped

71

by supernatural beings who labour on their farms. These beings are known as 'Zombi', and will do their masters' bidding at whatever cost. They may, for example, go out and steal for their masters, or commit other crimes. In addition, the Zombi are believed to have superpowers, such as being able to fly through the air at great speeds, or run faster than cars. The Haitian peasants believe that the Zombi are in fact reanimated dead people, who have been brought to life through magic spells and the power of potent drugs known as Wanga. These 'undead' beings will continue to do their masters' will for ever, labouring for hours on end in the fields and factories of the island. If, however, someone inadvertently gives them salt to eat on their food, they will suddenly realise who they are, desert their masters, and run off. They may even revisit the graveyard and try to get back into their graves.

INSANE WANDERERS?

According to Mars, these beliefs have no foundation whatsoever, but are ancient folkloric tales from Africa. He states in the paper, 'I have never met anyone in Haiti who was able to testify to me that he had seen a Zombi. However, I discovered afterwards that the hapless persons who were thought to be Zombis were, in fact, insane wanderers who could not identify themselves nor give any information with regard to their past life or their present condition. The unusual circumstances under which they appeared in the village, their queer behaviour and their unintelligible manner of speech,

induced the people, whose minds were already conditioned to superstition, to believe that Zombis were in town.'

Mars then goes on to give fascinating details of the Felicia Felix-Mentor case, which he personally became involved in. He recounts how, on the morning of 24 October 1936, there was a commotion in the remote village of Ennery, situated in the foothills of a mountainous region. A woman arrived in the main street of the village dressed in rags. She was elderly, and in a terrible state of decay and weakness. Her skin was scaly and pale, her eyes sore and red and her eyelashes missing. She seemed to have some kind of eye disease, and could not bear sunlight, and so had covered her eyes with a dirty rag. When questioned, she could give no answers as to where she had come from, and appeared not to understand what was said to her.

A ZOMBIE APPARITION

The people of the village became petrified, thinking that she must be a zombie. As they gathered around to look at the apparition, one of them recognised her as looking very similar to a member of the Mentor family, who lived close by. This was Felicia Felix-Mentor, who had died many years earlier. Accordingly, one of the Mentors was sent for, and the family removed the woman to their home, looking after her there before taking her to the government hospital. At this point, Mars himself, who was working for the Public Health Department at the time, was sent for to make an assessment of the woman's condition.

Mars reports how, under questioning, the woman was unable to report her name, her age, her place of birth or any other information about herself whatsoever. She had no knowledge of where she had come from or where she was going. She did speak, but in a nonsensical way that was impossible to understand or interpret. She occasionally burst into laughter, but there was no sense of enjoyment or mirth in these fits. She appeared indifferent to her surroundings, and had no sense of time.

WEAK AND MALNOURISHED

Mars went on to describe how, after careful supervision of the case, the woman grew stronger and began to look younger, changing her appearance from a woman of about sixty into one a decade younger. He also explained that he investigated the case thoroughly from all angles. The Mentor family had claimed that before the original Felicia died, she had suffered a fracture of the left leg, and was lame. They pointed to the fact that this woman was also lame. However, when Dr Mars took an X-ray of the woman's legs, he found that there were no fractures in either one. He attributed her lameness to the fact that she was extremely weak and malnourished, and had been limping as a result of muscular weakness. He pointed out that, as she gained weight and became more healthy, she stopped limping.

In conclusion, Dr Mars suggested that the unknown woman was suffering severe mental illness, probably schizophrenia, and that

the uneducated village people had mistaken this condition for that of a zombie from the grave. He added that the rural people of the island had many 'unscientific' beliefs about natural events occurring in their daily life and were apt, as a result, to indulge in mass hysteria when frightened.

MASS HYSTERIA

Moreover, Dr Mars mentioned the report of the folklorist and author Zora Neale Hurston, who had visited the island and brought back reports of zombies. Mars emphatically refuted the existence of such zombies, saying of Hurston, 'Evidently she got her information from the simple village folk, whose minds were conditioned to believing the real existence of a superhuman phenomenon. Miss Hurston herself, unfortunately, did not go beyond the mass hysteria to verify her information, nor in any way attempt to make a scientific explanation of the case.'

Mars also made a connection between the mass hysteria aroused by the Felicia Felix-Mentor case on Haiti and other instances of panics about supernatural beings in European culture. He says, 'Whole communities have been aroused into a mass hysteria as a result of unexpected appearances of queer persons. Such appearances very often rekindle the dying embers of archaic superstitious beliefs deeply rooted in the traditional culture of a people'. He goes on to express a wish that in the future, science may reveal such beliefs to be erroneous and destructive of the social fabric of our civilisation: 'Certainly, social psychiatry stands a good chance of exploding the Zombi-psychology of the untutored Haitian peasant, as well as any similar beliefs entertained in other cultures.'

ZORA NEALE HURSTON

Like the travel writer William Seabrook, Hurston was more interested in fiction than fact, and wanted to explore the powerful zombie myth in all its many contradictions, whether or not it was literally true.

Hurston was one of the leading figures of what was called the Harlem Renaissance, a time in the 1920s and 1930s when America produced a number of talented black intellectuals and artists who criticised the cultural mainstream and celebrated their own cultural identity. Among the writers associated with this movement were Hurston, Jean Toomer, Claude Mckay and Langston Hughes. Hurston jokingly referred to the intellectuals within the Harlem Renaissance, to whom she was loosely connected, as 'the niggerati'.

Hurston's most famous novel, *Their Eyes Were Watching God*, published in 1937, became known for its extraordinary rendition of black dialect, which she painstakingly recorded on field trips in and around the US and the Caribbean. Later, her work became unfashionable, as black intellectuals rejected what they saw as a negative characterisation of black people, but today, with the success of black women writers such as Alice Walker and Toni Morrison, she has once again taken her rightful place in literary history as one of the great chroniclers of the African diaspora.

Hurston was born in Notasulga, Alabama, in 1891, although she later claimed to have started life in Eatonville, Florida, where the family moved later. Eatonville was the first all-black town to be established in the US, and Hurston later described in a number of short stories and essays how living there gave her a positive view of her ethnicity from childhood. Her father became mayor of the town, and she grew up with a sense that black people were free to do as they pleased, irrespective of white society. However, when her mother died in 1904, she was sent away to boarding school. Her father then remarried, and when the couple stopped paying her school fees, she was expelled. She worked for a time as a maid, managed to get an education and went on to study at university, receiving a degree in anthropology from Barnard College, where she was the only black student. She worked with a number of leading anthropologists including Margaret Mead, was awarded some research posts and began to travel widely in the American South and the Caribbean for her work.

AN UNMARKED GRAVE

After a scandal in which she was accused of molesting a young boy, but defended herself against the allegations by saying that she was abroad at the time of the incident, Hurston found that she had to make her own way in the world once more. She became a freelance journalist, worked as a teacher and finally, was reduced to becoming a maid once more. Tragically, she ended her days in a welfare home, penniless and obscure, and was buried in an unmarked grave. It was only during the 1970s, when novelist Alice Walker and academic Charlotte Hunt took up her cause that she was rediscovered as one of the few female pioneers of African-American literature.

CONTROVERSY AND CRITICISM

Hurston's short stories, novels, and anthropological writings were unearthed and studied once more, including such important works as *Mules Men*, published in 1935, which detailed African-American folklore for the first time. Another study that came to light was *Tell My Horse*, published in 1938, an account of Vodun ritual in Haiti and African belief systems in Jamaica. Because Hurston was a fiction writer as well as an anthropologist, these were unique studies that were sensitive to the artistic content of the rituals and myths, as well as being significant field research.

Hurston was criticised by other writers of the Harlem Renaissance for failing to deliver a political message in her descriptions of black people, and for representing their speech patterns in a phonetic style, for example, using 'dat' for 'that', 'ole' for 'old', 'yuh' for 'you', and so on. For many years, this was regarded as racist. One of her critics was the politically motivated novelist Richard Wright, who called her evocation of black characters 'quaint' and said, rather unfairly, that her novels 'were not addressed to the negro but to a white audience whose chauvinistic tastes she knows how to satisfy.'

PROPHETIC WORDS

Hurston was also unwilling to align herself with the political left, speaking out against pro-communist sympathiser such as the poet Langston Hughes. She also opposed the idea of ethnically mixed schooling, arguing that black children would be better educated if they were separated from whites. This opinion was largely based on her positive experience of growing up in the black town of Eatonville. However, such ideas did not go down with the mass of left-leaning liberals, black or white, and she soon found herself marginalised, despite the fact that her writing was, on the whole, socially progressive. In retrospect, as Alice Walker and others have pointed out, Hurston was a strongly independent thinker, who refused to toe whatever party line was offered her, and paid the consequences for it by being more or less ostracised from American intellectual life in her later years.

In discussing the Vodun folklore beliefs and religious ceremonies of Haiti, Hurston made a perceptive remark that was later to be taken up by a number of scientists and medical researchers. She said, 'If science ever gets to the bottom of voodoo in Haiti and Africa, it will be found that some important medical secrets, still unknown to medical science, give it its power, rather than gestures of ceremony.' Her words were to prove prophetic.

THE CASE OF CLAIRVIUS NARCISSE

On 30 April 1962, a Haitian man called Clairvius Narcisse checked himself into the Albert Schweitzer Hospital, in the town of Deschappelle. He was coughing up blood and had hypothermia, digestive difficulties, lung malfunction and high blood pressure. A few days later, he died.

BURIED ALIVE

Clairvius' sister, Marie Claire, came in to the hospital to identify his body, and marked the death certificate with her thumbprint, which was the usual procedure in the hospital. He was buried on 3 May. However, eighteen years later, another of his sisters, Angelina, was walking through the marketplace at the village when a man approached her claiming to be her deceased brother Clairvius. He identified himself by using a childhood nickname that no one else would have known.

The man told her that when he was in the hospital, shortly before he had been pronounced dead, he had felt as though his skin was burning, and that insects were crawling about underneath it. Angelina herself recalled that before he visited the hospital, all those years ago, his lips had turned blue and that he had told her he had tingling sensations all over his body. Moreover, the man said, when the sheet had been pulled over his face as he lay motionless on the bed, he had been able to hear his sister crying. He said that throughout the entire process of burial, from being laid in his coffin to having it nailed shut, he had been entirely conscious, but because his body had been paralysed, he had been unable to move or cry for help. He even showed Angelina a scar that he said had been made from a wound, where a nail had been driven into his face while the coffin was being sealed.

Once underground, the man said that he felt as though he were floating above the grave. At this point, a bokor visited the graveyard, along with some assistants, and unearthed him. He was bound, gagged and beaten into submission, then taken to a sugar plantation in another part of the island, where he knew no one. Here, he worked for the following two years, labouring from dawn to dusk, along with other zombies who had found themselves in the same desperate situation.

ESCAPED ZOMBIES

One day, a fellow zombie turned on the bokor who was beating him and killed him, using a hoe. The group of zombies working for the bokor escaped, wandering the countryside and barely managing to feed themselves. Clairvius made efforts to contact his family for help, but his letters were never answered. He stayed away from his village for fear that his brother had arranged with the bokor to have him exhumed and enslaved. This was, Clairvius believed, a punishment for an argument he and his brother had had over some land. Finally, in desperation, Clairvius saw his sister in the marketplace, and approached her for help. She was horrified, and let out a scream, which caused a huge commotion. The case was reported all over Haiti, confirming to many the existence of what they had long believed: that some of the poorest and most exploited labourers in the land were, in fact, reanimated corpses – zombies.

SCIENTISTS MOVE IN

In 1982, the case was examined by two scientists: Dr Lamarque Douyon, the Director of the Haiti's Centre for Psychology and Neurology, and Dr Nathan Kline, a psychopharmacologist who had helped to set up the centre. Kline's work focussed on studying the psychological effect of various drugs. They began by considering whether to dig up the grave of Clairvius Narcisse, and in this way trying to establish the true state of the body. However, they eventually decided against this course of action, realising that the man claiming to be Narcisse might well have had the body removed, so as to support his story. Alternatively, if the man claiming to be Narcisse really was a zombie, another body might have been substituted in the grave, and given its state of decomposition, it would be impossible to tell whose it was. This was long before the era of DNA analysis, which can identify a person from the merest scrap of body tissue or fluid.

The researchers decided to question the man claiming to be Clairvius Narcisse, asking him about personal matters, such as his family history, and so on. According to their reports, the man amazed them by knowing all such details, which could not have been found out by any passing stranger. So convincing was his story that Kline decided to call in another scientist from America, to determine how it was that Clairvius Narcisse could have remained in a zombie state for so many years. Kline and Douyon suspected, as had Zora Neale Hurston, that the answer lay in the drugs administered by the sorceror who had apparently raised Clairvius from the dead. There was intense excitement at the prospect of finding out about a hitherto unknown drug that could induce a trance in a person for years on end, and many speculations on what such a pharmaceutical discovery might be used for.

In addition to talking to Clairvius Narcisse, the scientists also contacted a number of other individuals who had been rumoured to be zombies. However, in all these other cases, they found that the so-called zombies were in fact people suffering from serious illnesses such as schizophrenia, alcoholism or medical conditions such as epilepsy. Their alarming symptoms had terrified the simple peasants around them, who were unable to understand that the zombies were in fact unfortunate victims of illness. Narcisse's condition, however, could not be explained in such a way.

THE CLAIMS OF WADE DAVIS

The person called on to examine the Narcisse case was a young Harvard anthropologist and ethnobotanist called Wade Davis. Davis was Canadian, and had studied Biology, Anthropology and Ethnobotany at Harvard University. His particular interest lay in the uses of plants among indigenous peoples. He had spent several years in the Amazon and the Andes, living among tribes there and studying their customs.

GROUND GLASS AND SPIDERS' LEGS

On arrival in Haiti, Davis set about collecting his evidence. He bought specimens of the zombie powder from local bokors in different parts of the island. He found out that the bokors put a variety of strange items into their zombie powders, including parts of frogs, snakes, lizards, centipedes and sea worms. He also noted that in all cases, the powders included small pieces of human remains, such as ground bones and hair; plants containing skin irritants of different kinds; and a highly

toxic species of fish, the notorious pufferfish.

Davis discounted the human remains in the powder as having any effect in the process of zombification. He found that the skin irritants served to roughen and prick the surface of skin so that the victim would scratch him or herself, thus allowing the other elements of the powder to enter the body through the bloodstream. In some cases, he found bits of ground glass, or the legs of tarantulas, which would also have the same effect, of making the victim's skin itch.

Davis also interviewed the bokors themselves, finding out that in most cases, the bokors did not make the victims eat the powder. Instead, the powder would be put into the victims' shoes, or sprinkled down their backs. According to the bokors, the powder was not always effective, and if this proved to be the case, the victim might have to be sprinkled with it on several occasions before he or she went into a trance.

POWERFUL PUFFERFISH POISON

Davis's most exciting and controversial discovery was that the powder contained tetrodotoxin from the pufferfish. He noted that this highly toxic poison caused all the effects suffered by Clairvius Narcisse when he supposedly died. These included going blue at the lips, digestive problems, hypothermia, lung malfunction, high blood pressure and last but by no means least, paralysis of the entire body.

Davis knew about the severe nature of puffer-fish poisoning, of course. Tetrodotoxin is one of the most poisonous substances on earth, causing paralysis and death if ingested. It is located in the gut and reproductive organs of the fish, and if carefully removed, the flesh of the fish can be eaten, as it is in Japan, where the dish is known as *fugu*. In most cases, eating the properly prepared fish causes no more than a pleasant, euphoric sensation and a prickling of the tongue, but if any mistakes are made in the kitchen, the effects can be lethal. Individuals poisoned in such a way and revived have reported that while paralysed, they were completely aware of what was going on, and unable to alert those around them of the fact that they were not dead.

INTERRED IN A COFFIN

Davis's findings seemed to point to the fact that Narcisse had been telling the truth. Like the Japanese fugu victims, he had claimed that he had been fully conscious when pronounced dead, and had still been conscious when being nailed into his coffin. However, Davis could not explain why Narcisse appeared not to be suffering from brain damage. Anyone surviving being interred in a coffin would be likely to be severely brain damaged by the process. Davis also interviewed other people suspected of being zombies, including a young woman called Francina Ileus, and found that they were brain damaged, to the point of being virtually unable to communicate.

Davis also discovered that, as well as the zombie powder, the bokor used another weapon to subdue his victim. This was a preparation made with the infamous 'zombie cucumber'

containing a powerful hallucinogen called Datura (see page 40). Datura is known to cause confusion, psychosis, and in many cases, complete amnesia. He also remarked that, according to traditional lore, the zombie was given a salt-free diet to prevent showing any free will, and that this might induce a feeling of lethargy, especially in the high temperatures of Haiti's fields and factories.

AGGRESSIVE BEHAVIOUR

There were still many questions left unanswered, however. It is unclear how a zombie, reduced to a state of weakness, confusion and near paralysis, could be a useful slave to the bokor. In addition, there are many extremely poor people in Haiti, who will work for almost nothing, and so it is not difficult to find sources of cheap labour. Thus, the zombie legend remained a mysterious one, although Davis did make some progress in understanding its origins to some degree.

With his anthropological training, Davis was able to point to some aspects of the zombie myth that had not hitherto been considered. Using the case of Clairvius Narcisse as his evidence, Davis showed that the zombie myth stands as a warning to those who misbehave, and that the zombie traits of depersonalisation and loss of freedom are much feared in a culture where slavery was the norm for centuries. Exploring Narcisse's family history further, Davis found that this man had been a social pariah. He was selfish, aggressive and difficult. He had had numerous quarrels with many members of his family, and showed no thought for others. He had fathered many children and had refused to support them. He was also rich and successful by the standards of the rural area he lived in, in that he had managed to replace the thatched roof on his hut with a tin one. However, this success had come at the expense of his brother, who had a family to feed, and whose needs Clairvius had ignored. Clairvius had kept for himself land that was supposed to be shared with his brother, causing a bitter dispute between the two of them. In discussing these aspects of the case, Davis helped to show how the zombie myth had taken hold in Haiti, and discovered its function in maintaining order in small communities, as a sanction threatening social exclusion. To this extent, his findings were extremely insightful and useful.

THE SERPENT AND THE RAINBOW

Returning to the US, Davis sent samples of the zombie powder to a colleague, Leo Roisin of the New York State Psychiatric Institute. Roisin found that, when the powder was applied to the skin of rats, the rats showed symptoms of paralysis that were similar to that of fugu poisoning. Encouraged by what appeared to be vindication of his theory, Davis went on to publish his bestselling work, *The Serpent and the Rainbow*, which appeared in 1985.

The book met with much acclaim, fascinating the general public, and was translated into ten languages.

Readers were thrilled by the exotic locations, practises and rituals described, and Davis's arguments appeared to be persuasive. In particular, he showed how supposedly primitive cultures have their own knowledge of plant-derived drugs, and maintain a complex belief system in which these items are used, both medicinally and, sometimes, for the purposes of enlightening spiritual experience. In the case of the Haitian zombie, he demonstrated how the seemingly horrific folk beliefs of the islanders, in fact might help to maintain stability and social cohesion in times of extreme poverty and hardship, by acting as a sanction, thus ensuring that family members cared for each other and respected each others' needs.

Earlier, scientists such as Mars had seen nothing but superstitious belief in the myth of the zombie, and had regarded it as a pernicious, evil legend at that. Mars felt that such beliefs were a result of ignorance, and merely frightened poor village people who knew no better. He had criticised Zora Neale Hurston, the folklorist and writer, for believing the stories peasants told her. However, now it seemed that science and folklore had at last come together, in Davis' analysis of the Haitian zombie. On the one hand, Davis had uncovered the scientific facts of the matter; on the other, he had delved into the social significance of the zombie myth.

FROM SLAVE TO MONSTER

Over the course of the twentieth century, and into the new millennium, the Haitian zombie myth rapidly found its way into contemporary culture, appearing in films, comics, books and video games. However, through these mediums the Haitian zombie evolved into the gruesome horror zombie we are most familiar with today.

Firstly, in modern times, the element of the zombie's physical decay has been exaggerated to an extreme degree. Where, for example, Haitian 'zombies' such as Clairvius Narcisse or Felicia Felix-Mentor were reported to look ill, with staring eyes, blue lips, and pale skin, and were said to be confused as if drugged or half-dead, the modern zombie is described as a far more hideous being altogether. In the current legend, the zombie is a rotting corpse, with flesh coming away from the bones, so that parts of the innards or skeleton can be seen. There is a general focus on flesh and blood, especially the grosser aspects of these, and a fascination with the process of physical decay in the human body.

Especially for filmmakers, this gore-oriented aspect of the zombie legend has proved irresistible. Today, much of the zombie film genre concerns how much imagination and ingenuity the director can display in conjuring up utterly disgusting images of zombies. In some cases, this is done completely seriously, in an attempt to horrify and disgust the audience as much as possible. However, there may also be a very strong, humorous element in showing these revolting images. Today, zombie movies can range from glorifying gore to presenting a sophisticated parody of the horror genre – sometimes in the same film.

LUST FOR FLESH

Another major change from the creature of Haitian folk legend is the idea that the zombie has a lust for human flesh. While the Haitian zombie was the powerless slave of the bokor, and would carry out any task for his master, however cruel or violent, he did not, in most versions of the original story, live on human flesh and need to hunt it out in order to survive. The labouring peasant zombie of the cane field or factory ate a meagre, tasteless diet like other peasants, and it was only with the addition of salt to the diet that he or she would come alive. Even at this stage the Haitian zombie would not chase other humans, but would be more likely to run to the graveyard and try to get back into the grave. The Haitian zombie had no lust for anything, let alone human flesh. It was characterised by its lack of any human passions, whether love, pain or hatred.

TALES OF GORE

Thus, the idea of flesh-eating zombies, hungry for human bodies, is a fairly modern one, evidently invented to lend another gory aspect to the cinematic version of the legend. Not only does the rotting body of the zombie give the filmmaker a great deal of room for inventive photography, but also the ways in which the zombie attacks and eats his victim provides another opportunity to present as much gore as possible.

To an increasing degree, the popularity of the contemporary horror zombie movie depends on presenting ever-more ingenious ideas as to how to depict both the rotting 'undead' zombie corpse and its unfortunate victim. One of the most entertaining ways of doing this is to show the zombie slicing the top off his victim's head, putting its hand inside it, and eating the still-warm brains. Once again, this idea has no basis in Haitian zombie lore, but we can see why it would be an attractive concept to a filmmaker wanting to horrify and disgust their audience as much as possible, and why it therefore continues to be a popular theme in the modern cinematic zombie genre.

FROM TOILING PEASANT TO FLESH-EATING MONSTER

In other ways, too, the zombie has mutated from the humble, toiling peasant of the Haitian folk tale to the gruesome beast of contemporary cinema. The original zombie had tremendous strength, being able to withstand long hours of work under a boiling sun without complaining. This was because, without a soul, zombies were thought to be unable to feel any suffering, still less to lament their situation or try to escape. In some stories, the zombie was said to have certain supernatural powers, such as being able to fly very fast through the night, or being able to magically materialise somewhere without warning. On the whole, however, they were depicted as downtrodden labourers, only distinguishable from others by their seemingly superhuman capacity for hard work.

ZOMBIE SUPERPOWERS

In modern cinema, the zombie has developed an array of superpowers that make him a lethal opponent. The 'horror' zombie of today's popular culture never sleeps. It never gets tired, is impervious to pain, and requires no air to breathe. It is immune to drugs, to poisons, to gassing, electrocution, drowning, or virtually any other kind of attack. It can be shot and will not be harmed. In addition, it can suffer any kind of dismemberment or wounding without being destroyed. This is because the zombie is already dead, already a corpse. Most disturbingly, its head can 'live' without its body,

and vice versa. These traits, of course, make the zombie a terrifying monster, and once again provide the filmmaker or illustrator with innumerable opportunities for gross imagery or entertaining gags.

THE ZOMBIE APOCALYPSE

Another crucial addition to zombie lore in current times is the idea that a 'zombie apocalypse' is nigh. In this version of the myth, hordes of 'undead' zombies rise up from the grave, covered – of course – in gore, and hunt down the living, their one aim being to reduce the entire living population to the same status as themselves – miserable walking corpses – or simply to devour them.

This notion forms the basis of many zombie movies, and carries with it many themes, including the idea that the modern world reduces us all to automatons, or that we are all guilty of destroying ourselves and the planet through wars and industrialisation, so much so that we, too, will eventually be destroyed. With the current fear of climate change and the sweeping destruction it may carry with it, seemingly caused by our inability to stop the course of capitalism and curb our own greed, it is not surprising that the zombie myth, expressed in this way, should have become so popular in recent years. For many, it seems to address a central anxiety in modern civilisation: our destructive ways, and our lack of respect for the planet and for other human beings, will, eventually destroy each and every one of us too.

ROTTING CADAVER

In the modern zombie, we can see how the original traits of the Haitian zombie – a soulless, reanimated corpse who is slavishly devoted to a master and shows a capacity for unending work – have developed into a more exaggerated form: the zombie is now a rotting, decaying cadaver hungry for human flesh and impervious to any kind of attack. The horror zombie displays all the characteristics of a dead person, with a low rate of metabolism and a deactivated nervous system, but has a strong urge for eating human flesh, particularly the brains. Although it is clumsy with mechanical objects, it is extremely powerful. In addition, in some versions of the legend, a zombie can contaminate an ordinary human being with a single bite, thus transforming him or her into a zombie as well. In this respect, the modern zombie myth begins to echo that of the vampire or the werewolf. Indeed, in today's horror genre, the zombie has become just as important, if not more so.

As we have seen, the zombie legend of today is very much a creation of modern cinema. However, before the advent of film, there were versions of the story in literature around the world.

THE DEAD EAT THE LIVING

One of the first instances of this is a story in the ancient Sumerian poem, the *Epic of Gilgamesh*. It was here that the idea of the undead preying upon the living first came to be written down. The goddess Ishtar (who, in the Babylonian pantheon, is the goddess of fertility, love, war and sex) threatens:

I will knock down the Gates of the Netherworld
I will smash the doorposts, and leave the doors flat down
And will let the dead go up to eat the living!
And the dead will outnumber the living!

Evidently, the idea that the hordes of people who have died in the past may come back to wreak their revenge, is a very deep one in the human psyche. We see it in all kinds of stories of revenants, such as ghouls, vampires and other fiends. But this mention is also interesting because it pinpoints the idea that the many people who have died in the past far outnumber those living at any one time; so that, if they came back to destroy us, we would be completely overrun, and unable to offer any resistance. And, of course, the 'undead' are already dead; so not only are there more of them than us, but we cannot destroy them. All we can do, according to this nightmare scenario, is to join them.

CHILD-EATING DEMONS

Another forerunner to the modern concept of the zombie comes in the medieval Arabic collection of stories from the Middle East and South Asia, *One Thousand and One Nights*. In a story entitled, 'The History of Gherib and His Brother Agib', we learn of brave Prince Gherib who fights off a group of ghouls who want to eat him. Prince Gherib manages to convert them to his religion, Islam, and ends by enslaving them. What is significant about this story is that the ghouls are not simply there to frighten him; they wish to devour him, and he must fight for his life, or be drawn into their netherworld for ever. Muslim legend contains many other stories of ghouls, who are conceived of as malevolent spirits that like to eat human bodies, either stealing corpses or carrying off live children.

BODIES WASHED UP BY FLOODS

In eighteenth-century Europe we find a reference to the zombie myth in the work of the French historian Moreau de Saint-Mery. His book, *Description topographique et politique de la partie espagnole et de la partie francaise de l'isle de Saint-Domingue* was written between 1796 and 1798. It describes the customs and habits of people living on what we now call Haiti. In it, Saint-Mery mentions the Creole word 'Zombi', meaning a person who has come back from the dead. He suggests that this concept may have arisen when floods caused dead bodies to wash up from graves near the coastline of the island. He also describes the bokor, and the way in which the people believe him to have power over the land of the dead and an ability to capture souls.

FRANKENSTEIN: THE FIRST ZOMBIE?

The next zombie ancestor we come across is the famous *Frankenstein*, a tale written by Mary Shelley in 1818. Shelley was among a group of writers, artists and poets known as the Romantics. Romanticism dates from the second half of the eighteenth century, and was a complex European movement in art and literature. To some extent, in Britain, it was a revolt against the Industrial Revolution, which was swiftly changing the face of the countryside, turning the fields and woods of nature into what the poet William Blake called the 'dark Satanic mills' of the textile factories.

As a result of their horror of technology, the Romantics were more interested in the supernatural than in reason; just as in the medieval period, they were fascinated by the supernatural rather than what could be explained, and revelled in the gothic imagination, conjuring up ghastly tales of terrifying fiends. There was also a powerful strand within rationalism that represented the artists as tortured loners, misunderstood by conventional society. This idea continues to the present day and underlies many aspects of our popular culture, especially in the arts.

MORTALITY AND DECAY

In the figure of the zombie the fear of and fascination with the supernatural reaches its height. To believe in the horror zombie we are required to imagine that there is life after death and that, through our own guilt – whether through 'playing God' and meddling in the natural order, or merely through living on when others have died – the dead that we have buried can come back to life to haunt us. Not only this, but we must believe that these walking corpses have lost their souls and have therefore become violent, angry and vengeful. In addition, we must fear that they will eat us alive, reducing us all to the same condition that they have sunk to: half-eaten corpses, rotting and decaying. There is a significant parallel here between eating (consumption) and decay, and an overall revulsion at the physical nature of the human body. Moreover, the image of the horror zombie expresses a disgust at the physicality of the human body, vulnerable to death and the process of decomposition, but also to attack. Most disturbingly, there is a deep anxiety expressed that when we die we will not actually die but be condemned to a dreadful half-life, in which we will be permanently maimed.

Taking its cue from the zombie of Haitian myth, the depiction of the horror zombie of today's popular culture, especially in zombie films and games, plays with these ideas, alternately amusing and disgusting us with its ever more outlandish fantasies of how the human body can be eaten, either by the natural forces of decay, or by avenging hordes of undead monsters from the grave. There is, of course, a humorous element in all this, but it can also be a deadly serious reflection on mortality.

THE LEGEND OF FRANKENSTEIN

Mary Shelley's novel *Frankenstein*, published in 1818, told the tale of a monster who was created from a reanimated corpse, much like a zombie. However, unlike the zombie of Haitian myth, this monster was able to think, feel, and express emotion. While *Frankenstein* is not strictly a zombie, many features of Shelley's story found their way into the depiction of zombies in popular culture; most importantly, the idea that a monster can be created by a scientific process.

A VIOLENT MONSTER

This was a new idea, since before Shelley's day, the creation of monsters had typically been imagined as a mystical process involving divine or Satanic intervention. In Shelley's story, the monster has been made by a scientist, Victor Frankenstein, who creates a being that he cannot control. This monstrous semi-human turns out to have incredible strength, and to be extremely dangerous, committing several murders. However, unlike a zombie, Frankenstein's monster has a heart, and possibly a soul – he needs human company, in particular, he needs a female partner, and is very lonely because he is shunned by humanity and has no companion.

Shelley's novel, with its central figure of a pseudo-human being created by science, was a dire warning about the dangers of technology. The Romantics were extremely suspicious of modern technology, and to a certain degree, with good reason: the Industrial Revolution sweeping Britain was destroying many of the old ways of life, pushing rural communities into the factories, and ravaging the countryside. Shelley's tale of a beast created by technological wizardry stood as a symbol of all that the Romantics feared and hated about the process of industrialisation, and issued a timely warning that scientific progress could eventually spell the destruction of mankind.

MEDDLING WITH NATURE

Perhaps one of the reasons that the tale of Frankenstein became so popular in the years that followed, creating a whole horror genre around it, is that this message is still so relevant. Today, we are reminded of Shelley's warning as industrial development becomes increasingly out of control, threatening to unbalance the natural world, in the shape of climate change, to an unprecedented degree.

Mary Shelley's warning not to meddle with the natural order – in particular, not to play God by trying to create human beings – was rooted in European folklore, where the idea of the revenant was central. Stories of the dead returning from the grave to wreak revenge upon the living abound in these ancient folk tales. The revenants take different forms, as vampires, ghouls, demons, werewolves and what we now call zombies – soulless 'undead' beings with the outer form of human individuals.

THE 'LIVING DEAD'

What characterises all these revenants is a desire for revenge: to make the living pay for their deaths and to take them down into the miserable hell that they, as the 'living dead', are forced to endure. As we have seen from the Sumerian poem of the Goddess Ishtar, this is an age-old concept that is evidently a deep-rooted part of the human psyche. It seems that in many cultures, at many different times in history, people have expressed their guilt at living on when others have died, whether loved ones or enemies, through stories about the dead coming back to claim the living and dragging them down into the underworld. There is also a sense of horror at the idea that when we

die we may live on in an eternal purgatory. This is a notion derived from Christianity, from the concept of Hell, and may also be an inversion of the more positive religious promise of eternal life in Heaven.

THE ZOMBIE CHILD

The tale of Frankenstein was not the only literary work to influence the modern zombie horror genre. In 1902, English writer W. W. Jacobs published a short story entitled, *The Monkey's Paw*. In it, a man and his wife mourn the death of their young son. The man then comes across a magic monkey's paw that will grant him any wish he desires. Naturally, he wishes for his son to come back, but when the son returns, he does so in a decayed form. This, as can be imagined, is a nightmare for all concerned, and eventually, the man wishes for his son to return to his resting place in the grave. The story ends with the son dying, and the man and his wife coming to terms, at last, with their beloved child's death.

Both *Frankenstein* and *The Monkey's Paw* are sad, affecting stories that deal with a central issue in human experience: that of losing a loved one. Mary Shelley's story was written after she gave birth to a premature baby who later died. Shortly afterwards, she recorded in her journal: 'Dreamed that my little baby came to life again – that it had only been cold and that we rubbed it before the fire and it lived.' Some critics have argued that this experience of loss led Shelley to write *Frankenstein*, and that the novel was an attempt to address the issue of procreation and her ambivalent feelings about motherhood.

'PLAYING GOD'

In *The Monkey's Paw* we again find the theme of a loved child who has died. Both stories indicate clearly that, however much we may want to take creation into our own hands, whether it be giving birth to a new human being or bringing a loved child back to life, terrible consequences may ensue if we do. It is interesting to speculate what both of these authors would have thought of genetic engineering in the present day, and how they would have reacted to the process of cloning, or to the possibility of creating human beings 'to order', with high intelligence, good looks and so on. One can only imagine that they would have been horrified by such developments, and would regard our contemporary scientific world as evidence of human beings 'playing God', with results that might prove catastrophic for the human race.

'EVIL ALTOGETHER'

Another precursor to the zombie horror film is to be found in the work of the science-fiction/horror writer H. P. Lovecraft. Lovecraft was influenced by nineteenth-century American writers such as Edgar Allan Poe, who wrote many tales of the supernatural, and Ambrose Bierce. In the story *The Death of Halpin Frayser* Bierce told of the way in which people who died could come back from the dead, transformed into vengeful, spiteful beings. Their loss of a soul would make them purely

evil, without any good or merciful qualities. The narrator in the story says:

'Whereas in general the spirit that removed cometh back upon occasion, and is sometimes seen of those in flesh (appearing in the form of the body it bore) yet it hath happened that the veritable body without the spirit hath walked. And it is attested of those encountering who have lived

to speak thereon that one so raised up hath no natural affection, nor remembrance thereof, but only hate. Also, it is known that some spirits which in life were benign become by death evil altogether.'

LOVECRAFT'S 'ZOMBIES'

Lovecraft takes up this theme of the vengeful undead in a number of his short stories and novelettes, including *The Thing on the Doorstep*, *The Outsider*, *Cool Air*, *Pickman's Model* and *In the Vault*. (This last story was significant in that it featured a character who was actually bitten by a zombie, perhaps the first instance of this in Western literature). However, it was Lovecraft's short story, *Herbert West – Re-animator*, which was serialised in the amateur publication *Home Brew* in 1922, that proved the most memorable of his zombie creations.

This story was a definitive one, and is considered to be a milestone in the creation of the modern horror zombie. In it, Lovecraft describes the zombie as a walking corpse who has been reanimated by scientific means, and is an entirely mute, brutal, violent and heartless creature. This characterisation of the zombie has remained the prototype of the horror genre, particularly in the films of George A. Romero and other later interpreters.

HERBERT WEST – THE ORIGINAL 'MAD SCIENTIST'

The plot of the story is long and complicated, since it was published in several episodes. However, one plot line reveals a doctor who tells of a colleague, Herbert West, who views the human body as a machine that, once dead, could be 'restarted' if given the right chemical injections. West performs various unpleasant experiments on animals to test his hypothesis, but ultimately comes to the conclusion that he must use humans.

At first, he uses corpses robbed from graves, but this does not work as the bodies have been dead too long. Then he manages to acquire a recently dead corpse, of a labourer who died that morning in an accident. The injections are given, but nothing happens until, in the dead of night, there is an unearthly scream. The doctor and West flee the house, tipping over a lamp that sets fire to the house. The house is burned to the ground and with it, they assume, the corpse. However, the next day, they read in the paper that there are claw marks on the grave of the recently deceased labourer. As with the Haitian zombie, the reanimated corpse has evidently been trying to get back into the grave for a little peace and quiet.

ZOMBIES FROM THE CATACOMBS

The next episodes in Lovecraft's series deal with West's ever more gruesome attempts at reanimation. He does actually manage to do this, but creates a violent man who embarks on a killing spree and is eventually committed to a mental institution. In another episode, a boxer is reanimated, only to stalk the town, kidnap a child and eat it, while another tells the tale of a decapitated World War One doctor who comes to life.

In the final episode of the series, *The Tomb Legions*, Lovecraft tells the gruesome tale of the undead bursting out of the catacombs and disembowelling West, also decapitating him, in revenge for all the suffering that this mad scientist has inflicted on them in pursuit of his dream of reanimation.

MERCILESS GHOULS

Although Lovecraft did not refer to the undead in his story as 'zombies', as vengeful, violent and merciless ghouls from the grave they had all the hallmarks of the zombie myth, and went on to inspire numerous zombie comic and films. Indeed, the first episode was later adapted in EC Comics *Weird Science* in 1950. In this way, Lovecraft can be seen as the forerunner of the popular zombie horror genre.

However, Lovecraft himself was not very happy with his Herbert West stories. He commented that they were a parody of Mary Shelley's *Frankenstein*, citing the poetry of Samuel Taylor Coleridge as another inspiration, and said that he only wrote them for the money. (He was paid US$5 per instalment.) One of his chief criticisms of the West series was that each episode had to start with a recap of the previous episode and to end on a cliffhanger, which he found foreign to his way of writing. Nevertheless, the stories went on to become extremely popular, and today Lovecraft is credited with 'reanimating' the zombie legend for future generations of science fiction/ horror writers and filmmakers.

GALVANISM – SCIENCE OR FICTION?

Many of these writers were influenced by developments in science, in particular the idea of galvanism. In biology, the term galvanism is used to denote the contraction of a muscle that has been stimulated by an electric current. It first came about in the late eighteenth century, when a scientist called Luigi Galvani had conducted experiments on dead frogs, dissecting them and applying electrical currents to their bodies to see if he could find out how their muscles worked. He discovered what he called 'animal electricity', and believed that he had found a particular form of electricity derived from animals.

Galvani's colleague, another eminent scientist of the day, Alessandro Volta, came to a different conclusion, however: that the two pieces of metal holding the frogs' legs in Galvani's experiment were themselves interacting to make electricity, and that the leg was merely acting as a conductor. Volta went on to invent the electric cell, now known as the battery. For his part, Galvani's theory was disproved, causing a bitter split between the two scientists. Today, the study of the effect in biology that he discovered is known as electrophysiology, and the term that bears his name, 'galvanism', is only used in a historical context.

ELECTROCUTING CORPSES

Horror writers have always looked to new discoveries in science for gruesome ideas in telling tales of the undead. Mary Shelley was no exception. She is known to have used some general ideas from the science of her day in her novel *Frankenstein*. In particular, she consulted Humphry Davy's *Elements of Chemical Philosophy*. (Davy was a highly imaginative and popular scientist of the day, who is still remembered as the inventor of the Davy Lamp, a safety lamp used by miners underground.) During the period Shelley was writing, there was immense excitement and interest in the new discoveries of science; and this fascination continued into the nineteenth and early twentieth centuries.

Many Victorian scientists were convinced that if electricity was applied to the brain of a human corpse in the correct fashion, it would come back to life. A great deal of energy was expended in this fruitless enterprise, which nevertheless continued to excite the public imagination. Thus, early science fiction/horror writers such as H. P. Lovecraft drew on an age-old aspiration in science, from the alchemists of medieval times, to the electrical experimenters of the Victorian age: unlocking the secret knowledge of how to reanimate dead bodies and bring corpses back to life.

Even today, the dream still has not died, with believers in the ability to freeze and reanimate bodies through cryogenics, along with all manner of other theories. However, to date, science has not been able to reanimate dead bodies – thankfully enough, if we believe the warnings of writers such as Shelley, Bierce, Lovecraft and the zombie filmmakers of our own era.

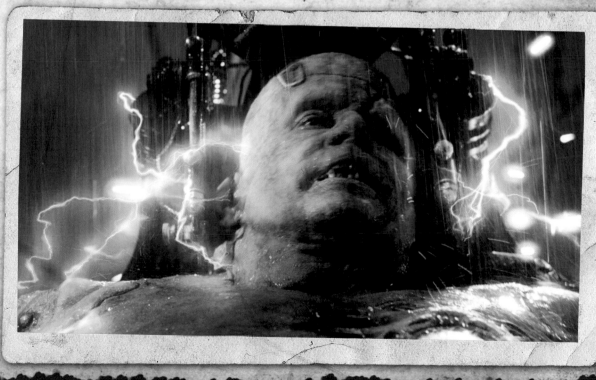

WHITE ZOMBIE

As we have seen, by the turn of the twentieth century, zombies had become a feature of horror, mystery, and science fiction stories in popular horror literature. However, the zombie had not yet made its way into the world of cinema. The first zombie movie to hit the screens was *White Zombie* in 1932, a film which set the benchmark for the enormous numbers of zombie movies that followed.

SHE WAS NOT ALIVE ... NOR DEAD ... Just a

WHITE ZOMBIE

Performing his every desire!

A VICTOR & EDWARD HALPERIN Production

with BELA *Dracula* LUGOSI

Released by UNITED ARTISTS

MURKY CHILLERS

Written by Garnett Weston, a Hollywood screenwriter whose career had begun with a film called *The Viking*, it was directed by an independent team, Victor Halperin and his brother Edward. What made *White Zombie* stand out from many other horror films of the period, and is still distinctive today, is the subject matter: the Haitian zombies of lore and legend. It drew some influence from the Broadway play, *Zombie*, by Kenneth Webb. After the release of the film, Webb sued the Halperin brothers, claiming that they had copied his play, but he lost his suit, since the film differed in many important respects from the stage play.

The director of *White Zombie*, Victor Hugo Halperin, who often collaborated on his films with his brother Edward, had a reputation for making low-budget romance and horror movies. He began his career in the cinema as a jack-of-all-trades, working as an actor, producer, writer and director. His first notable film as a director, *Party Girl*, starred Douglas Fairbanks, the well-known matinee idol, but after that he moved on to gothic horror, releasing a string of cheaply made, murky chillers during the 1930s. They were variable in quality and distributed by many different companies, ranging from large distributors such as Paramount to very obscure organisations. Halperin ended his working days as a director at PRC Studios and then seems to have disappeared. His death went unremarked. Today, the best known of his films is *White Zombie*, starring Bela Lugosi, and an unusual film called *A Nation Aflame*, released in 1937, an anti-racist expose of hate groups such as the Ku Klux Klan. (Strangely, the film was based on a story by Thomas Dixon, the controversial author of works such as *The Clansman*, but it carried the opposite political message).

FACTORY ZOMBIES

White Zombie tells the story of an evil voodoo bokor, Murder Legendre, who turns a white woman into a zombie. The bokor is played by Bela Lugosi, in a characteristic role as a threatening, evil man whose cryptic remarks are punctuated by long silences. The role of the beautiful young victim is taken by Madge Bellamy, an actress who had made her name in the silent movies of the twenties. The film tells the story of Madeleine Short and her fiancé, who are about to be married. They go to stay with a friend, a wealthy plantation owner named Charles Beaumont, who is secretly in love with Madeleine. While the couple are there, Charles goes to visit Murder Legendre, who has seen the guests travelling on the way to the plantation and appears to have evil intentions towards them. Murder runs a sugar-cane mill manned by an army of zombies, who work tirelessly for their corrupt master. Charles wants Madeleine to fall in love with him and asks Murder to perform some magic spells for him that will make this happen. Murder tells him that in order to do this Charles will first have to give Madeleine a magic potion that will turn her into a zombie. Charles agrees and manages to slip the potion to Madeleine. The effect of the potion is delayed, but eventually she succumbs, and becomes a willing victim.

ZOMBIE TRANCE

Before the potion takes effect, Madeleine and her fiancé marry, but not long after the ceremony, Madeleine dies. She is buried in a tomb on the island, to the grief of her new husband, who takes to visiting it often. During the night, Murder and Charles steal her body away from the tomb and reanimate her as a zombie. However, the fiancé, Neil, visits his dead wife's tomb and finds her body gone. He enlists the help of a local missionary, Dr Bruner, to help find it. Bruner tells him of Murder's terrible trade in zombification, and the two

men set out to rescue the hapless Madeleine.

Meanwhile, Charles himself also finds himself turning into a zombie as the result of Murder's evil potion. When Neil and Bruner arrive, Murder orders Madeleine to kill her husband. Madeleine tries to do so, brandishing a knife, but Bruner manages to save him. Murder then sets his other zombies on Neil and a fight takes place on the edge of a cliff. Bruner knocks Murder out, breaking his telepathic hold on the zombies, who fall to their deaths over the cliff edge, jumping over one by one, like lemmings. Murder, too, eventually suffers the same fate. His death releases Madeleine from her zombie trance, and husband and wife are once more reunited.

MIXED REVIEWS

The making of *White Zombie* was a rather ramshackle affair, with money borrowed from different sources. Much of it was shot at Universal Studios, using props and effects borrowed from other horror films. Bela Lugosi was the star, having had a major success in the film *Dracula* the year before. Most of the rest of the cast, including the leading lady, were fading stars. Reports about Lugosi's behaviour on set varied; Madge Bellamy found him polite and respectful, noting that he kissed her hand every day when she arrived on set; others, however, including the cameraman, criticised him as unfriendly. Madge Bellamy was also viewed with mixed feelings. Over the years, she had gained a reputation for being difficult to work with, because she led a wild life of going to all-night parties, which left her tired and bad-tempered in the daytime.

Despite all these problems, the brothers finished the film, and it opened in New York as planned. Initially, it got bad reviews from the critics. They panned its unlikely storyline and poor acting and viewed it as childish and old-fashioned. Others opined thus: 'The film is only interesting in measure of its complete failure'; and 'So earnest is it in its attempt to be thrilling that it overreaches its mark all along the line and resolves into an unintentional and often hilarious comedy.' However, audiences did not agree, and it was a box-office success, performing particularly well for an independently made film.

REVOLT OF THE ZOMBIES

In modern times, the film has, in general, been more positively viewed. Most agree that it has serious flaws, specifically in the acting, which is generally held to be one of its weakest aspects. However, Halperin's vision of Haiti and the evil underworld of the voodoo master is also praised as original, poetic, and atmospheric. The entire film seems to take place in a dreamy, disoriented version of the zombie trance, introducing images of innocence, corruption, death and spirit possession, in an ambitious, stylised fashion that perfectly captures a sense of foreboding and threat, and also references many themes from folklore and fairy tales. According to one critic, the director's ideas of the film were complex and fascinating, but the actors were unable to deliver performances that interpreted them in a believable way.

Halperin went on to make a sequel to the film, entitled *Revolt of the Zombies*, starring Dean Jagger rather than Bela Lugosi. This was released in 1936, but it did not fare well. In most critics' estimation, it was deeply inferior to *White Zombie*, with none of the spark of its predecessor.

WHITE ZOMBIE: THE LEGACY

Today, *White Zombie* has made its mark as the first true zombie movie. It is seen as a forerunner of the dark, brooding horror films of Val Lewton in the 1940s and has earned itself a place in cinema history as a flawed masterpiece of its time. Sadly, most of those involved in it did not make movie history again. Halperin dropped out of sight towards the end of his film-making career and was never heard of again. Bela Lugosi went on to star in a series of badly made, low-budget movies that are generally considered to be second rate. (When he died, he was buried in his Dracula costume, which had represented the high point of his career.) Madge Bellamy's film career continued to decline, until in 1943 she was tried for attempting to shoot a wealthy lover, Stanwood Murphy. In her defence, she said, 'I only winged him, which is what I meant to do. Believe me, I'm a crack shot.' The scandal, which revealed that she was having an affair with a married man, effectively ended her career. However, after living in poverty for many years, she finally died a rich woman after selling property during a real-estate boom, and commented that this transaction had made her more money than she had earned in her entire film career.

Years later, in the 1980s, an American heavy-metal rock band, White Zombie, kept the name of the film alive, also using some of its themes to inspire their songs.

ZOMBIE APOCALYPSE

The next milestone in the history of zombie movies was the film *Things To Come*, released in 1936. The screenplay was written by the well-known British science fiction writer and political thinker H. G. Wells. In the story, inhabitants of a war-torn London become infected by a disease called 'wandering sickness', reducing sufferers to a zombie-like trance which leaves them aimlessly and mindlessly walking around.

PREDICTION OF WAR

Things to Come was an adaptation from Wells' earlier novel, *The Shape of Things to Come*. Wells was an influential figure in Britain at the time, and has since come to be recognised as one of the founding fathers of the science fiction genre. He wrote several novels set in the future, often beginning with catastrophes that break up the old order and usher in the new. In *The Shape of Things to Come*, published in 1933, he predicted the outbreak of World War One, imagining that whole cities would be bombed from the air by warplanes. This was tragically prophetic, but the next episode in the story was not: he fantasised that the world would be ruled by a council of scientists.

ZOMBIE DISEASE

This is the story that forms the basis of director Alexander Korda's film, *Things to Come*. For the screenplay adaptation, Wells also introduced ideas from his political writings. The tale begins in 1936 and ends a hundred years later. We are introduced to the main character, John Cabal, a successful businessman who lives in Everytown, which is modelled on London. On Christmas Day, he and his friends Harding and Passworthy discuss news of the impending war, disagreeing as to its likelihood and effects. That night, there is a bombing raid on the city where they live and global warfare erupts. Cabal becomes a fighter pilot, and many adventures ensue, but the war drags on for decades, plunging humanity into a primitive state of existence, suffering outbreaks of a mysterious disease called 'wandering sickness'. The effects of this disease mean the sufferers forget who they are and simply walk around in a zombie-like state.

A NEW WORLD ORDER

In order to combat this problem a warlord ordered all those infected to be shot. This frightening scenario, of a zombie apocalypse, was the first of its kind on screen, and made a very deep impression on its audience, who were also stunned by the groundbreaking special effects in the film, particularly in the futurist sequences.

The desperate situation of a zombie apocalypse and the meltdown of modern civilisation continues, in the film, for decades until the 1970s, when Cabal flies in to Everytown, proclaiming that he has come to save mankind. He and a band of scientists, engineers and mechanics have been building a rival civilisation in another country and are intent on forming a world council to preserve peace. The new organisation is

called 'Wings Over the World', and has renounced war as a means of bringing its aims to pass. The warlord, however, is not impressed by Cabal's rhetoric and promptly takes him prisoner. Inevitably hostilities between the two sides break out. Cabal's followers bomb the city with sleeping gas, killing the Chief, and finally win the day. As Wings Over the World is proclaimed the victor, the new order begins.

The film then fast forwards to the new millennium, with a montage showing the rapid technological achievements of the twentieth century and beyond. Wells imagined that by 2036 human beings would be living in underground cities with every kind of modern convenience at their disposal. However, as the story goes on to show, not everyone is happy in this utopia. A band of opponents of the system, led by a sculptor, claim that progress is unfolding too fast and demand a halt to it. The conflict eventually comes to a head over a proposed manned flight to the moon. As the rebels threaten to destroy the spaceship, the grandchildren of Cabal and Passworthy rush to make sure the flight will go ahead and finally manage to outwit the anti-progress lobby.

At the end of the film, Cabal makes a memorable speech putting forward his idea that the nature of mankind is to seek knowledge, to pursue progress and that if this noble aim comes to a halt we cease to be fully human and may as well live out our lives as animals. In his opinion, we human beings are not seekers of happiness and rest, but have a compulsion to find out more

about the world, whether or not this brings contentment. Cabal equates 'rest' with 'death' and says, 'But for Man, no rest, no ending. He must go on, conquest beyond conquest. First this little planet with its winds and ways, and then all the laws of mind and matter that restrain him. Then the planets about him, and at last, out across immensity to the stars. And when he has conquered all the deeps of space and all the mysteries of time, still he will be beginning.'

INFECTED BY PLAGUE

The film was significant in its portrayal of a world taken over by primitive, zombie-like human beings with no respect for the more refined aspects of life, such as culture and knowledge, and no tender human emotions, like love, pity and mercy. It dealt with a wide range of other issues as well, such as the outbreak of war and technological progress (especially in warfare), and because of its breathtaking special effects it was a landmark science fiction movie of the period.

In terms of the zombie genre, *Things To Come* proved a major influence in putting forward a notion that became central to the zombie legend: the idea of a plague infecting mankind and causing havoc to such a degree that civilisation breaks down, leaving a horde of wandering people living at the most primitive level. Wells's nightmare scenario of the sick preying upon those still able-bodied enough to protect themselves and their families among the ruins, is one that later became a staple of the zombie horror movie. In addition, Wells prophesied the complete breakdown of society on a global scale, and emphasised the global nature of the future economy and political situation. In many ways, his predictions have come to pass, though, thankfully, the more macabre apocalyptic elements have to date remained in the province of science fiction.

I AM LEGEND

Where *White Zombie* introduced the idea of the zombie factory, in which mindless automatons labour for an evil capitalist master, *Things to Come* brought in a rather more frightening idea: the notion of a zombie apocalypse produced by a worldwide plague, reducing civilisation to the Dark Ages once more. In addition, there was one more important work of fiction that added another aspect to the zombie horror genre, and that was Richard Matheson's *I Am Legend*, published in 1954.

The novel tells the now-familiar story of a lone hero battling against a disease that turns the human race into violent, aggressive, flesh-eating monsters. These monsters are, in Matheson's story, a type of vampire. However, the story later became incorporated into the zombie legend when George Romero, director of the seminal *Night of the Living Dead*, remembered the impact that the novel had had on him. Commenting on his film, he said: 'My script grew out of a short story I had written, which was basically a rip-off of the Richard Matheson novel.' He then added, 'I used zombies instead of vampires; I always thought that zombies were a sort of blue-collar, working-class monster that

might show up in anybody's back yard.' Another idea that was inspired by Matheson's novel was that of showing the world as it collapsed, rather than beginning the film in the aftermath of apocalypse, which is more common. In Matheson's story, the vampires besiege the hero's house, until they surround it, leaving him to fend them off as best he can. This aspect of the story had a great impact on Romero, who later said, 'I ripped off the siege and the central idea, which I thought was so powerful – that this particular plague involved the entire planet'.

NIGHTMARE SCENARIO

In retrospect, we can see how these stories – Halperin's *White Zombie*, Wells' *Things to Come*, and Matheson's *I Am Legend*, touched on fears that were – and in some cases, still are – central to our modern civilisation in the Western world. Halperin's *White Zombie* conjures up a world where human beings are reduced to automatons, as a result of modern technology: our fear of losing our souls is expressed here, as is our fear of the unknown, of difference. In Wells' futuristic vision, a global plague wipes out centuries of progress and civilisation in a single blow, in a scenario that could have been written today, as we react with anxiety to each new prophecy of pandemic, whether it be SARS, bird flu or any number of other diseases that move and mutate so swiftly as a result of modern communications. Matheson's nightmare scenario conjures up our worst fears about how quickly civilised life can descend into chaos, bringing out our most aggressive, violent impulses as we struggle for survival. It is no coincidence that *I Am Legend* was written at the time of the Cold War, when the tensions between East and West threatened to end in the destruction of the entire mass of humanity, at the touch of a button. The novel was a great success and, as well as influencing Romero's *Night of the Living Dead*, was adapted into three films: *The Last Man on Earth* (1964), *The Omega Man* (1971) and *I Am Legend* (2007).

Above: Scene still from *The Omega Man*, Boris Sagal, 1971. Based on the 1954 novel *I Am Legend*.

TALES FROM THE CRYPT

In the years after World War Two, young male adults began to take a tremendous interest in a new form of reading entertainment: the horror comic. Wearied and disillusioned by the experience of the recent global conflict, whether as soldiers or civilians, the American male population in general were no longer enthused by adventure stories and tales of heroism: they wanted sex, violence, and horror in their fiction, and — if possible — graphic depictions of all of these, in as tasteless a form as possible.

BLACK HUMOUR

The publishing company Educational Comics, started by Max Gaines in the 1940s, was known for such titles as *Picture Stories from the Bible.* Two years after merging the company with DC Comics in 1944, Gaines died in a boating accident. His son, William Gaines, inherited the business, and soon changed its direction, to supply the new demand for horror comics. The company's name was switched to Entertaining Comics, and Will Gaines began to focus on horror, science, military and crime fiction. His editors Al Feldstein and Harvey Kurtzman recruited a highly talented group of artists including Johnny Craig, Reed Crandall and others. The magazines also pioneered such features as Letters to the Editor and the Fan Club, building up a relationship with their readers that helped to make the various titles very popular.

The company went on to publish a series of notorious horror titles, including *Tales from the Crypt,* *The Vault of Horror* and *The Haunt of Fear.* These stories, featuring supernatural creatures such as ghouls, zombies and werewolves, were imaginatively illustrated by original, highly skilled artists, using innovative techniques that in many cases derived from film: for example, the 'film noir' aesthetic, using dramatic light and shade effects. Not only were the illustrations modern and daring, but the storylines were also subversive in their way – hard-hitting and ironic, with a black sense of humour and often rather surprising twists at the end.

THE CRYPT KEEPER

As well as the horror titles, EC also published war tales such as *Frontline Combat,* and the science fiction series *Weird Science,* but these, too, were light years away from the heroic stories of pre-war comic books, tackling issues such as sex, racism and drug use. The stories were told in a comical way, and the defining characteristic of EC's output as a whole was the sophisticated mix of gruesome gore and sardonic humour. In later years, filmmakers such as Romero and others used this same potent recipe of graphic horror and zany comedy to present the horror zombie on screen.

In *Tales from the Crypt*, a character called The Crypt Keeper introduced and commented on the stories, cracking sick jokes and bringing a light-hearted element to the proceedings. Front covers were often absurdly lurid: for example, a sexy young woman would be shown in the arms of a cadaver dripping with blood, on a one-way journey down into the underworld. Other characters known as Ghoulunatics were also brought in as part of the show: these included The Old Witch and The Vault Keeper, who entertained readers by sniping at each other, also in some cases making disparaging remarks about the readers themselves. The stories were original, breaking the mould of the old fashioned adventure tales, and introducing teenagers to a quick-witted, dry humour that they soon made their own. Since those days, it is clear that much teenage and young adult-oriented comedy has built on these twin features of grossness and ironic humour. Thus, the EC horror series were ahead of their time, in a most remarkable way.

MORAL OUTRAGE

The lurid illustrations and bizarre plots of EC's output may seem harmless enough to us now, but at the time they attracted intense moral outrage. The comics, with their striking, original illustrations and irreverent, gruesome storylines were seen as having the power to corrupt a rising generation of young Americans. Articles with titles such as *Horror in the Nursery* were penned by child psychologists, while media commentators ran headline stories about the terrible effects such reading matter could have on teenagers, making them rebellious, violent and depraved. One psychologist, Dr Fredric Wertham, even wrote a paper in a learned journal entitled, *The Psychopathology of Comic Books*.

Before long, teachers, parents, religious leaders and child specialists rose up as one to condemn the comics. All manner of social ills, such as 'juvenile delinquency', which was seen as a pressing problem in America at the time, were attributed to the reading of such material at an early age. The comics were also held to be responsible for high levels of illiteracy among the youthful population. This was a strange piece of logic, since one would think that having exciting reading material would motivate children and teenagers to read avidly, rather than the reverse.

In 1954, a committee called the Senate Subcomittee on Juvenile Delinquency was asked to consider the comics' terrifying assault on the delicate sensibilities of American youth. In their report, they did not go as far as blaming the comics entirely for the outbreak of bad behaviour among American teenagers, but they did raise the issue, and ask that the publishers of such comics tone down the violent, gruesome element.

By all accounts, the publishers, finding it difficult to know what to do in this situation, were unable to respond. Finally, Gaines hit upon the idea of calling a meeting and forming a publishers' body of their own, which they duly did. This was known as The Comics Magazine Association of America, and there was also an allied body, The Comics Code Authority. Unfortunately, in a move EC Comics had not foreseen, this organisation started to issue draconian edicts as to the content of the comics, eventually forcing many publishers out of business.

CENSORING THE COMICS

Ludicrous as it may seem today, comic books and magazines were no longer allowed to use the words 'horror' and 'terror' in their titles. The illustrators were also forbidden to depict gruesome scenes, or to show supernatural creatures such as zombies, werewolves, ghouls and the like. Not surprisingly, this dealt a death blow to EC's line of horror comics, and in 1954, the director of the company, William Gaines, cancelled the publication of *Tales from the Crypt* and the companion horror titles on his roster.

Today, it is hard to believe that such tame material could have provoked such an extreme moral reaction, and even harder to credit that the publishers of these lucrative comics would have capitulated so easily to this kind of pressure on the industry. However, that is what happened, to the great disappointment of many young readers who had been thoroughly enjoying the series and who had never shown any signs of juvenile delinquency whatsoever.

In retrospect, it seems that the real reason for the outcry was a panic reaction to some of the problems that were beginning to beset America

in the 1950s, in particular that of 'juvenile delinquency'. During this period of American history, there was an enormous pressure to conform, and any signs of independence or rebelliousness on the part of the youth were ruthlessly quelled. Partly because of the Cold War fear of Communist invasion, there was a pervasive fear of any type of liberal or left-wing criticism of American ideals, and a sense of paranoia that the rising generations were being corrupted by anti-establishment views.

LEGACY OF THE CRYPT

It is certainly true that some of the EC Comics stories, whether horror or science fiction, were highly critical of the repressive ideas and cultural values of the American dream in the 1950s, as it was presented by the government and the authorities of the period. For example, in one science-fiction story, *Judgment Day*, a human astronaut visited a planet of robots divided into two races according to their colour, red or blue. One of the races is given special privileges, while the other has no rights at all. After realising that the division is only made on the basis of colour and has nothing to do with the robots' respective skills or talents, the astronaut realises that the system is completely unfair. Then, in the final twist, when the astronaut removes his helmet, we find out that he is in fact a black man.

The story was written as a comment on racial bigotry in America, but the publishers were ordered to delete the image of the black man and substitute it for a white man. Legend has it that there was an angry telephone conversation between the Comic Code Administrator, Judge Murphy and EC editor Al Feldstein, along with the magazine's publisher, Gaines. After a heated exchange, Feldstein and Gaines refused to do what Murphy told them and left the artwork as it was, eventually running the story in its original form in an issue called *Incredible Science Fiction* (number 33).

However, in the end, EC Comics lost the battle against the moral majority. It soon became clear from the *Judgment Day* debacle that the days of the company were numbered. Eventually, all the horror and science fiction titles, including *Tales from the Crypt*, were closed down. For many years, the company limped on, badly damaged by the unfair censorship of the early fifties. However, it later revived, with the publication of the highly successful teen-oriented magazine *Mad*.

Today, there have been many attempts to revive the *Tales of the Crypt* series, some successful, others less so. These include reprints of the comics, and adaptations for film and television. The HBO series *Tales from the Crypt* commenced in 1989 and continued for the next ten years, with over ninety episodes. A follow-up series entitled *Perversions of Science*, based on the science fiction rather than horror stories, was not so popular and was cancelled after only ten episodes.

NIGHT OF THE LIVING DEAD

Despite the demise of the *Tales of the Crypt* horror comic in the early fifties, the legend lived on and the series has been continually revived in many forms: print, television and film. But perhaps the most significant tribute to the original was George Romero's film *Night of the Living Dead*, made in 1968. Shot in black and white on a very low budget, this independent movie nevertheless became a classic.

ZOMBIE HORDES

The story begins as a brother and sister (Johnny, played by Russell Streiner, and Barbra, played by Judith O'Dea) drive across country in Pennsylvania to visit their father's grave. In the graveyard, a hideous zombie appears and tries to carry Barbra away. Johnny fights the monster, but is killed. In terror, Barbra tries to make her getaway in the car, but is forced to abandon it after crashing it into a tree. She finds a farmhouse and decides to hide there from the zombie. However, she soon realises that there is a pack of zombies who are trying to force their way in. When a man called Ben (played by black actor Duane Jones) arrives at the farmhouse, it soon becomes clear that hordes of zombies are intent on destroying them both, along with the rest of the living. Ben destroys several of the zombies, setting them on fire. He boards up the windows and doors of the house,

scaring off the zombies surrounding the house by putting a blazing chair on the porch. Meanwhile Barbra, who is traumatised by the death of her brother and these ensuing events, collapses into a catatonic state and is unable to move.

Later, it emerges that other people are hiding in the cellar of the house: a couple called Tom and Judy and a family, Harry, Helen and Karen Cooper. Karen Cooper is unwell, having been bitten by one of the zombies.

MASS MURDER

It then transpires that the attack of the zombies is not simply a localised problem, but that mass murder has been breaking out on a grand scale in the area. Through radio and television reports, Ben finds out that the zombies, all of them recently deceased corpses, have been coming to life and killing hundreds of people. They are motivated by an intense hunger for human flesh,

and are especially keen to devour brains. Citizens are advised to shoot the ghouls when they see them, or hit them hard over the head. The authorities have tried to reassure the population that armed patrols are keeping the situation under control, but this is not very persuasive.

Matters take a turn for the worse when Karen, Harry's daughter, reveals herself to have become a zombie as a result of the infectious bite she received from one of the ghouls. To the horror of her mother, Helen, she begins to eat her father's corpse. When Helen tries to stop her, she stabs her mother with a trowel, eventually killing her.

TRAUMATISED CHILDREN

The film was not, initially, well received. It was first released on 1 October 1968 at the Fulton Theater, Pittsburgh, and thereafter was shown as a Saturday afternoon matinee. The audience was mainly adolescents and children. In those days, there was no proper film rating system, so young children were allowed to buy tickets. In many cases, they were not accompanied by their parents. Obviously, *Night of the Living Dead* was completely unsuitable for such children, and completely traumatised them. This was no ordinary horror film. Its depictions of flesh eating were graphic, and the whole scenario absolutely terrifying, rather than enjoyably scary. In addition, there was no resolution or closure at the end: the hero simply perished, along with everybody else.

Not surprisingly, given its subject matter, there was little serious criticism of the film at first. It provoked a certain amount of controversy because of the gruesome nature of some of its scenes, but few critics took notice of it. However, it soon became a box office success, outperforming all other independent horror films of its type. Over the next ten years, it earned up to US$30 million at the box office, and was released in Europe, Canada and Australia. It was also translated into more than twenty-five languages. In 1999, it was added to the National Film Registry of the Library of Congress, becoming one of a select group of movies judged to be 'historically, culturally or aesthetically important'.

ORGY OF SADISM?

Because of its success at the box office, reviewers were forced to take *Night of the Living Dead* seriously, but even so, many of them dismissed it. Some described it as socially irresponsible, others called it 'a junk movie', and it was also described as 'an unrelieved orgy of sadism'. However, there were influential commentators, such as Pauline Kael, who saw it as 'one of the most gruesomely terrifying movies ever made'. Critic Rex Reed added, 'If you want to see what turns a B movie into a classic ... don't miss *Night of the Living Dead*. It is unthinkable for anyone seriously interested in horror movies not to see it.'

After a while, it became clear that, although the matinee screening of

LEFT: Scene still from *Night of the Living Dead*, George A. Romero, 1968.

the film was undoubtedly a bad idea, the film itself was remarkable. Not only was it absolutely terrifying – no mean feat in an outlandish sci-fi tale of zombie apocalypse and other unlikely happenings – but it was also, some critics argued, a serious and deeply subversive commentary on American politics and culture. Writing in *The Village Voice*, critic Elliot Stein spoke of the film as a commentary on the horror of the Vietnam War, which was a hugely controversial issue at the time: 'This was middle America at war, and the zombie carnage seemed a grotesque echo of the conflict then raging in Vietnam.' Film critic Sumiko Hagashi pointed to the way the film was shot, in grainy black and white, using a similar technique to the often highly disturbing newsreel footage of the war.

NIHILISTIC FLAVOUR

Other critics pointed to the racial aspect of the film. George Romero, the filmmaker, refused to admit that there was any political significance in making Ben, the hero of the film, a black man. However, critics noted that the ending of the film, in which the hero dies, might have been a comment on the assassination of black leaders such as Martin Luther King and Malcom X, while the way in which Ben dies – tragically, and unfairly, killed by a redneck posse – mimicked the lynchings of black men that were still taking place in the South at that period. In addition, critics alluded to the deeply nihilistic flavour of the film in general, which may have been provoked by the horrifying carnage in Vietnam and the American government's seeming unwillingness or inability to terminate the war in any just or fair way.

Not everyone admired the film, however. As well as those who criticised what they saw as sensationalism and sadism, there were feminist commentators who disliked the fact that all the women in the film were portrayed as helpless and weak. The main female character, Barbra, is in a catatonic state of fright during most of the film, while others such as Judy and Helen make serious errors of judgement. Moreover, by the end of the film, all of them are dead.

THE SPIRIT OF THE SIXTIES

The filmmaker himself, George Romero, has warned against reading too much into the movie. As he sees it, the film captured the spirit of the times. The sixties was a rebellious period for many young people, who believed that here, for the first time, was an opportunity to change the course of history in order to create a better, more just society. As Romero put it himself: 'It was 1968, man. Everybody had a message. The anger and attitude and all that's there is just because it was the sixties.'

Romero has also acknowledged the influence of EC Comics' *Tales from the Crypt* and the sci-fi classic *I Am Legend* by Richard Matheson on his ideas for the film. Indeed, the film more or less copies the Matheson scenario, with the hero barricading himself into a house and fighting off hordes of evil undead (in this case zombies rather than vampires). Thus, *Night of the Living Dead* mines a rich seam in American horror fiction, and with its terrifying tale of a zombie apocalypse, has taken its place among the classics of the genre.

THE ROMERO ZOMBIE

George Romero's *Night of the Living Dead* was innovative in many ways, introducing a new form of horror zombie to a rising generation of cinemagoers. The 'Romero Zombie', as the film's zombie monsters became known, was a very different breed from the traditional zombies of Caribbean folklore. These were no longer poverty-stricken labourers, but large lustful cadavers with a slow, shuffling walk.

WARM BLOOD AND BRAINS

One of the main reasons that the Romero zombie is so frightening is that it is almost impossible to kill them. Limbs can be chopped off, but this will not stop the zombie from chasing a live human being. The Romero zombie has a fiendish desire for fresh human flesh, in particular, warm blood and brains, and will stop at nothing in pursuit of these. Even when the zombie is decapitated, the head may still present a danger, and can sometimes still bite once it is severed from the neck.

The Romero zombie is also fearless, and immune to pleas for mercy. The only phenomenon that frightens it is fire. However, this does not mean that the Romero zombie can necessarily be destroyed by being burned. Moreover, the Romero zombie feels no pain, and therefore will not suffer in the least when set alight. Thus, it is unclear how best to kill the Romero zombie.

THE INFECTIOUS BITE

Another defining characteristic of the Romero zombie is that, like the vampire and werewolf of medieval legend, its bite is infectious to live human beings. Once bitten, an ordinary person will, over time, turn into a ravening monster, hungry for human flesh. In Romero's film, one of the characters, Karen, turns into a zombie as a result of being bitten, and thinks nothing of eating her dead father's remains and beating her mother to death so that she can feast on her as well. In this way, Romero emphasises that the zombie has lost its ability to empathise with human pain, to love, or to feel any kind of sympathy for others.

HOW TO KILL A ZOMBIE

In *Night of the Living Dead*, it is never made entirely clear why the zombies have come back from the grave to wreak their revenge on the living. Various theories are advanced, for example that radiation from a failed space probe has been released into the atmosphere, causing the reanimation of corpses buried underground. Another explanation that is hinted at is that the zombie hordes have been unleashed as a result of black magic, or that zombification comes about as the result of a plague or other type of pandemic. Alternatively, the zombies could be explained as a species of alien, sent from another race to conquer and destroy the planet earth.

The mystery surrounding the phenomenon of the zombies adds to the sense of fear and danger in the film, as does the notion that nobody knows exactly how to deal with them. Romero envisages small posses of vigilantes as a way of combating the zombie apocalypse, and shows the zombies being burned on a funeral pyre as a way of stamping out the plague. However, by the end of the story, we do not know whether this is effective. We are unsure as to whether the human race will survive the zombie massacre – we only know that Ben, our hero, has been thrown on the funeral pyre alongside one of the monsters.

DARK AGE OF CARNAGE

Neither do we understand how the zombies hope to survive – whether by eating human flesh, until it runs out and they are forced back underground, or by somehow halting the decomposition of their bodies, which are rotting even as they stalk the earth in search of victims. All we know is that the zombie apocalypse is a nightmare vision, in which any last vestiges of human civilisation are swept away – along with humane ideals such as love, pity and mercy – and all that remains in its place is a long, dark age of violence, carnage and horror.

BESTIALITY, GREED, AND LUST

Although terrifying on screen, in reality the idea of a zombie apocalypse may seem somewhat absurd to any rational person. However, once we begin to look at *Night of the Living Dead* as a critique of the Vietnam War in particular, and even war in general, the notion of civilisation being replaced by bestiality, greed and lust, does not seem so very outlandish. While Romero has resisted political interpretations of his work, one cannot help but see the Romero zombie presented in *Night of the Living Dead* as a caricature of the greedy American capitalist, whether businessman or consumer, destroying its victims across the globe, eating them up in a never-ending quest for greater consumption and eventual world domination.

Various theories have been advanced as to the popularity of the Romero zombie as a modern monster that is even more frightening than its revenant predecessors (for example, the vampire, the werewolf, and the Caribbean zombie). Firstly, of course, the Romero zombie evokes a strong fear of death, in particular, the body-specific characteristics of the recently deceased corpse. None of us like to imagine ourselves after death, lying underground, rotting away as a cadaver, with worms and insects eating our bodies. How much more horrifying is it to think that such a corpse might rise up from the grave and walk around, trailing blood, gore and maggots, shuffling from place to place as best it can using a rapidly decomposing body.

FEAR OF DEATH AND DECAY

This image, of course, has connections to our experience, as human beings, of old age – whether that of our loved ones or ourselves. It is a profoundly disturbing experience to witness the decay of our bodies as we grow older, accompanied not only by pain, but by severe limitations on our daily activities. George Romero's graphic depiction of the body in all its horror in *Night of the Living Dead* is one of the reasons that the film was, for many people, so memorable, focusing as it did on our fear of death and decay, and bringing to mind the carnage resulting from modern warfare.

In addition, the Romero zombie expresses our fear of contagion. This theme is a central one in *Night of the Living Dead*, since the zombie plague spreads through infection from a bite. Since the 1960s, when the film was made, the fear of global pandemics of all kinds has increased: not only of AIDS, but of various kinds of viral infections, from SARS to bird flu to swine flu. The Romero zombie, with its infectious bite, carries on the traditional idea of a plague being spread by revenants from the grave, which was particularly prevalent in the middle ages, and spawned such imaginary monsters as vampires and werewolves.

ISOLATION AND ABANDONMENT

Night of the Living Dead also tells another profound story, that of humanity's fear of isolation. As in Robert Matheson's *I Am Legend*, the hero of the tale finds himself cut off from the rest of humanity, fighting a lone battle against a race of evil monsters. The hero is alone, fearing himself to be among the sole survivors of the human race, unable to contact his fellow human beings, and prevented from calling on their help. This, of course, speaks to a very deep-rooted anxiety in all of us, that in most cases springs from our earliest experiences in childhood, when we fear that, small and helpless as we are, we may be completely cut off from others, including family and loved ones, and may be left to fend for ourselves in an alien, uncaring, or – in this case, positively threatening – world. This theme shows itself again and again in horror and science fiction, and continues to provoke terror, even among the most sophisticated and worldly audiences.

As well as our fear of being excluded from the love and care of other human beings, *Night of the Living Dead* concerned our equally profound anxiety about the possibly evil motives of those around us. In the film, there are two zombies who are loved family members: the first is Barbra's brother, Johnny, and the second is Karen, daughter of Harry and Helen Cooper. Both of these people turn into zombies, Karen with hideous results, as she turns upon her mother and father. Underlying our need for others is a fear that they mean us harm, and will destroy us. In this way, the film accesses secret but often strong childhood fears about parental and sibling love, or lack of it, and the way that families can harbour murderous emotions towards each other under the guise of close relationships.

ZOMBIES: FRIGHTENING OR FUNNY?

Last, but not least, the Romero zombie presents us with a phenomenon that is not only terrifying, but in some ways, extremely funny. There is always a thin line between what is gross and what is amusing, and *Night of the Living Dead* exploits this territory in a skilful fashion, with images that are at once gruesome and absurd. In the same way, people experiencing dreadful events, such as terminal illness, war, plague and so on, or simply living through the ordinary stages of life such as ageing and watching elderly relatives reach the end of their lives, may indulge in a kind of black humour as a means of emotional survival. Looked at from this angle, the Romero zombie is not only a terrifying monster, but – with its shuffling gait, its decaying body, and out-of-control desires – a comical parody of the human being, seen from the point of view (albeit somewhat exaggerated) of our most unpleasant and unattractive physical and mental attributes as members of the human race.

GEORGE A. ROMERO'S

DAY OF THE DEAD

LEGACY OF THE DEAD

Besides introducing the Romero zombie to cinema audiences, thus providing a ghoulish new character in the modern horror pantheon of vampires and werewolves, *Night of the Living Dead* also paved the way for a slew of low-budget zombie movies. Romero showed that even with severely limited funds, intelligent and hard-hitting horror films could be made, and in this way, the genre was thrown open to a huge number of inexperienced filmmakers.

Nicknamed 'Grandfather of the Zombie' because of his groundbreaking film *Night of the Living Dead* and its sequels, George Andre Romero was born on 4 February 1940 in New York City to an immigrant family. His mother was Lithuanian and his father Cuban-American. His father was employed as a commercial artist, and the young Romero also went on to work in the field of the visual arts.

After graduating from Carnegie Mellon University in Pittsburg, Romero began work as a TV and film director, mostly directing commercials. He formed a company called Latent Image with friends John Russo and Russell Streiner. (Russo would later go on to write the screenplay for *Night of the Living Dead*, and also took a small role as a zombie in the film. Streiner also helped to produce the film and played the role of Johnny, who is killed by a zombie and later returns as a zombie himself.)

LOW-BUDGET HORROR

One of Romero's early jobs was to direct a segment of *Mister Rogers' Neighbourhood*, a children's TV series hosted by Fred McFeely Rogers, a well-known educator, minister and songwriter. This series was extremely successful, second only to *Sesame Street* as the longest running children's show on PBS (Public Broadcasting Service). In the episode Romero worked on, he had to film a person having a routine operation, and found this aspect of filmmaking so intriguing that he decided to make a speciality of it and enter the business of making horror movies.

Together with friends and associates, Romero formed a new production company, known as Image Ten. His friends Russo and Streiner were also involved in this venture. Each of Image Ten's associates then contributed around US$10,000 to fund the company's first full-length feature film, *Night of the Living Dead*. In total, the budget reached US$114,000 – not a great deal by industry standards.

From these humble beginnings, the movie went on to become one of the most celebrated horror films of all time, marking the entry of the modern 'horror zombie' onto the cinema screen, and has since become a classic of the genre.

Because the budget for the film was so small, there were many limitations on how it could be shot. The producers realised that they could not make a horror movie on the model of classic films that they had seen as children and adolescents – their tiny budget precluded that. So, instead, they decided to use an ordinary location, using a remote farmhouse in the Pennsylvanian countryside, and let the bleak landscape, rather than special effects or complicated sets and backdrops, provide the threatening atmosphere. The crew also shot footage in a cemetery. In addition, they shot indoor scenes in a regular town house, and basement scenes in another house near a local park.

BOSCO CHOCOLATE SYRUP

The special effects and props used in the movie were mostly homemade and improvised. In particular, liberal use was made of Bosco Chocolate Syrup, which was poured onto the actors' bodies to resemble blood. The syrup had been used before, as fake blood in the famous shower scene of Alfred Hitchcock's *Psycho*, a film released in 1960 that went on to become a classic. (Many years later, artist Vik Muniz created a copy of Leonardo Da Vinci's 'The Last Supper' made entirely in Bosco Chocolate Syrup, which fetched over US$100,000 when it was sold.)

Romero's movie was shot on 35mm black and white film. Once again, this decision was made in order to save money. However, this limitation ultimately worked in the movie's favour, since the cheap film gave it a grainy quality rather like a wartime newsreel. The quality of the filming was later described by movie historian and producer Joseph Maddrey as 'guerrilla style'. He described *Night of the Living Dead* as being 'like a documentary on the loss of social stability' rather than a typical exploitation movie.

When it came to distribution, the producers of the film met with almost unanimous opposition. Nearly all the distributors wanted to cut the gory, explicitly violent scenes, and substitute a happy ending for the desolate final scene in which the hero is burned to death on a funeral pyre alongside one of the zombie monsters. However, Romero and his crew remained adamant that the ending, and the gore, should stay. Finally, a distributor was found who agreed to show the film uncut and uncensored.

SPLATTER AND PORN

Such was the success of *Night of the Living Dead* that George Romero went on to direct six sequels. The film also paved the way for what later became known as the 'splatter film' (a term coined by Romero himself), describing a particular type of horror film in which gore and violence are the major visual themes. The focus in these films is on the wounding and mutilating of the human body, often presented in a highly theatrical way. Some critics see such films as merely exploitative, dependent on the cinemagoer's voyeuristic and sadistic fascination with blood and guts. Others are more sympathetic, viewing them as intelligent, original and even groundbreaking forms of modern art in their disregard for the ordinary values of storytelling and visual presentation. Perhaps the answer lies somewhere in between, in that such films, while provoking our curiosity and morbid interest in gore, may also sometimes offer an incisive critique of modern society, especially the greedy, warlike and amoral aspect of capitalism. In addition, we should be aware that, in many of these films, the gore is not to be taken too seriously: when carried to extremes, it can often, and quite intentionally, become a device for surrealist comedy.

In a subgenre of the so-called 'splatter films' (themselves a subgenre of the horror movie in general), there is often an excessive interest in sadistic or masochistic sex. Where this is involved, such films have been labelled 'gorno' movies (a combination of 'gore' and 'porno') Once again, we might view these films as profoundly disturbing and highly exploitative, or simply see them as playful forms of entertainment, often ironic and quite sophisticated in that the visual gags may mimic more serious movies, perhaps sending them up. Some commentators have argued that such films in fact show more integrity than the 'soft porn' of the typically Hollywood blockbuster, in that there is no attempt to present the themes as anything more than what they are – that is, sensationalist, and usually tongue in cheek, entertainment.

HORROR IN SUBURBIA

Perhaps the most important legacy of *Night of the Living Dead* was in making the 'ordinary' a place of terror and horror. As a result of the film, locations such as parks, cemeteries, and ordinary suburban neighbourhoods began to be seen, for the first time, as places where the supernatural could lurk, whether in the shape of a zombie, vampire, werewolf or other unearthly creature. In previous eras, horror films had always been set in exotic locations such as Transylvanian castles and remote European forests. Alternatively,

they might be given lavish historical settings, attracting audiences to the cinema as much to see the costumes as to witness the drama. The low budget of *Night of the Living Dead* changed all that. After its release, it became clear that menace of a different kind could be evoked by setting the drama in an ordinary house, street or neighbourhood. Indeed, the idea that evil could lurk behind the façade of the suburban

Above: Film poster from Night of the Living Dead, George A. Romero, 1968.

house and garden, with its white picket fence, gave the horror story an enjoyably terrifying contemporary twist.

NIGHTMARE OF MIDDLE AMERICA

In the wake of Romero's *Night of the Living Dead*, other directors began to make powerful horror films using real locations and shooting on a low budget, instead of assuming that complex special effects and sets were needed to create the right atmosphere. In the decades that followed, directors such as John Carpenter, Sean Cunningham and Wes Craven set terrifying films in quite ordinary locations. Films such as *Halloween*, *Friday the 13th*, and *Nightmare on Elm Street* all followed this pattern, with tremendously successful results, drawing inspirations from Romero's groundbreaking idea of bringing horror, terror and evil to the ordinary streets and houses of middle America.

In 1990, director Tom Savini released a remake of *Night of the Living Dead*, using the same title as the original. The screenplay had been rewritten by George Romero. In general outline, the story was much the same as the first film, but there were significant alterations: for example, the character of Barbra, who had been presented as weak and mentally unbalanced in the original film, became stronger and more resourceful. Romero produced the film, and Savini, who was known for his skill at special effects and horror make-up, directed it. Initially, it received poor reviews – maybe because on first watch it seemed that not much had changed from the original – but has since been regarded in a more sympathetic light as the great B-movie re-make that it is.

DAWN OF THE DEAD

The sequel to *Night of the Living Dead* was released in 1978. Entitled *Dawn of the Dead*, it took a different direction from the previous movie, presenting a horrific scenario of a zombie apocalypse as a worldwide plague. Romero's trademark mix of gore and satire remained and some critics felt that the film was more ambitious than the first.

HORROR IN THE MALL

The story begins as we learn that a pandemic has broken out across the world, somehow causing the dead and buried to become reanimated. (How this has actually happened remains a mystery, adding to the sense of confusion of the plot.) Unfortunately for the living, the zombie revenants stalk the earth, preying on live human beings as a source of nourishment. As the human race looks set for extinction, a handful of survivors come together in a shopping mall and are besieged by zombies, barricading themselves in and trying to stop the onslaught of the hideous monsters.

What the film had in common with its predecessor was that the location was an ordinary, everyday one: in this case, a suburban shopping mall. Once again, the budget for the film was low, although not quite as low as that for *Night of the Living Dead*.

A GORY FEAST

In the film, four people – a TV reporter, a helicopter pilot and two military men – manage to keep the zombies at bay for a while, using the mall as their base. The shopping mall has been abandoned as a result of the zombie plague. Full of consumer goods, the four survivors are able to indulge their every whim, but of course, this lust for material objects becomes meaningless in a world where civilisation has broken down and there is nothing more to hope for.

Eventually, a gang of bikers break into the mall, which results in the zombies also getting in. Instead of banding together, the bikers and the mall survivors begin to fight, which allows the zombies to take advantage of the situation. The bikers are eaten by the zombies, in a gory feast that made the film notorious. Then one of the survivors, Stephen, who has been bitten, reanimates as a zombie. He leads his zombie friends to the rest of the gang, but two of them, Francine and Peter, manage to escape, flying off in a helicopter which is about to run out of fuel.

ALTERNATIVE ENDING

According to some reports, Romero had not planned this ending. In true nihilist style, and never one to miss an opportunity for gore, he wanted a desperate finale, in which Peter, the helicopter pilot, shoots himself in the head, while his girlfriend Francine puts her head into the helicopter blades and slices it off. However, the producers of the movie felt that this would be too unpopular and so the ending was changed. But in the cut that remained, there were hints that both the lead characters, in the final moments of the film, were suicidal: Francine stands on the roof of the building for some time, doing nothing to save herself as the zombies approach, while Peter actually puts a gun to his head before deciding to change his mind and make a bid for freedom with Francine.

A 'RELENTLESS EXPLOITATION OF GORE'?

The film was first shown in New York on 20 April 1978, and initially attracted criticism from religious and social groups. For example, the United States Conference of Catholic Bishops Office for Film and Broadcasting commented: 'George Romero's camp pulp yarn has metaphorical pretentions as a social satire, but essentially what's on the screen, peppered with rough language, is a relentless exploitation of gore and violence and the repulsive effects of violence'. Whether or not such pronouncements helped to attract curious audiences to the movie is not known, but *Dawn of the Dead* went on to do very well at the box office. The fact that there was a striking advertisement campaign trumpeting the movie as 'the most intensely shocking motion picture experience of all time' may have helped. Today, the film is considered to be one of the most most successful of all Romero's zombie movies.

The reviews of *Dawn of the Dead* (also known, in some countries, as *Zombi*) at the time of its release were both positive and negative, sometimes in one and the same review. For instance, critic Roger Ebert wrote that it was 'gruesome, sickening, disgusting, violent, brutal and appalling', but he also declared that it was 'one of the best horror films ever made' and gave it a top rating of four out of four stars, commenting that 'nobody ever said art had to be in good taste'. Another critic, Steve Biodrowski, saw the film as 'a savage (if tongue-in-cheek) attack on the foibles of modern society'. He felt that it was wider in scope than its predecessor, envisioning a global apocalypse and the total breakdown of civilisation rather than just a localised outbreak of mayhem. He also admired the production values of the film, adding: 'The acting performances are uniformly strong, and the script develops its themes more explicitly, with obvious satirical jabs at modern consumer society, as epitomised by the indoor shopping mall where a small band of human survivors take shelter from the zombie plague sweeping the country.'

GRISLY EVENTS

However, there were some critics who hated the film, particularly the gory aspect, which they felt detracted from any notion that it had serious criticisms to make about modern society. Critic Janet Maslin walked out of the cinema after a quarter of an hour, commenting that she had a 'pet peeve about flesh-eating zombies who never stop snacking'. A critic in *Variety* magazine also disliked the relentless gore, writing that the film 'pummels the viewer with a series of ever-more-grisly events – decapitations, shootings, knifings, flesh tearings – that make Romero's special effects man, Tom Savini, the real 'star' of the film.' The critic added, 'Romero's script is banal when not incoherent'.

Despite these criticisms, *Dawn of the Dead* went on to become one of the classic horror movies of the 1970s, greatly influencing its successors. Today, it is viewed by many critics and commentators as an extremely sharp social satire, a searing indictment of materialism in contemporary America. By setting the action in a shopping mall full of consumer items, surrounded by the mayhem of a zombie apocalypse, Romero appears to be saying that our habit of taking refuge in material goods as a way of shutting out the madness of modern life is doomed to failure. Another reading of the film is that the rich, symbolised by the survivors in the shopping mall, want to barricade themselves in, away from the poor, symbolised by the 'walking dead', the zombies. Interestingly, this reading takes us back to the origins of the zombie myth in Caribbean folklore, which tells of toiling peasants being reduced to working for the master, or bokor, as slaves (see page 16).

BRIGHT RED BLOOD

As well as entertaining viewers with its combination of gore and satire, *Dawn of the Dead* fascinated movie buffs because of its production values. The film was shot at the Monroeville Mall, which Romero had visited with a friend whose company managed it. Romero's friend, Mark Mason, had joked that if someone wanted to hole up in the mall in the event of an emergency, they would be able to survive for quite a long time there. This apparently set Romero thinking, and he subsequently came up with the idea for *Dawn of the Dead.*

One of the most important aspects of the film was the make-up for the zombies. This was done by a well-known make-up and special effects

artist, Tom Savini. Savini organised a small crew to apply zombie make-up to a cast of several hundred extras for the film, painting their flesh a blue-grey. In addition, he managed to give the impression of an exploding head by casting one of the actor's heads, filling it with pieces of food, and shooting it so that it exploded. The fake blood in the film was bright red, which apparently Savini disliked, but Romero felt would add a 'comic book' feel to the movie. Today, critics admire the dream-like quality that this obviously fake blood gives to the atmosphere of the film.

THE ZOMBIES SPEED UP

In 2004, a remake of *Dawn of the Dead* was released (below). Directed by Zack Snyder, the film was positively received on the whole, but critic Roger Ebert, who had been extremely admiring of the original, felt that the new film was not as witty or sharp. One of the aspects of the remake that differed from the previous version was that, where Romero's zombies lumbered around slowly, Snyder's zombies came at their victims fast and furiously, baring their teeth like animals. Romero himself was critical of this development, and some critics pointed out that the speed at which the zombies moved in Snyder's film meant that their make-up did not have to be too cleverly detailed. In addition, the idea that these creatures were 'undead', retaining some characteristics of a corpse, was lost, so that the zombies did not have such a terrifying impact. However, despite these cavils, the 2004 film did well at the box office, helping to establish Snyder's career as a mainstream director.

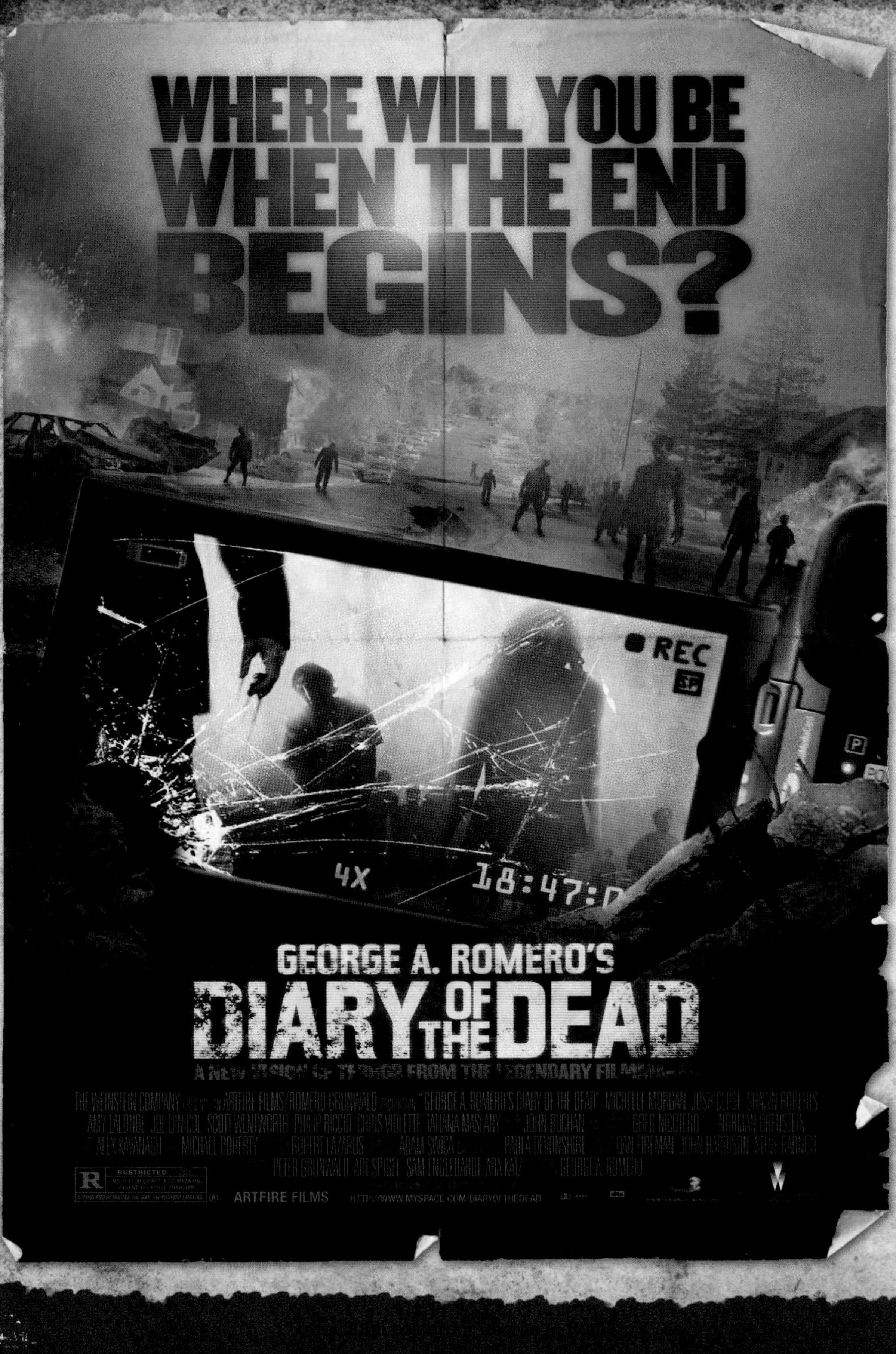
WHERE WILL YOU BE
WHEN THE END
BEGINS?
REC
SP
4X
18:47:0
GEORGE A. ROMERO'S
DIARY OF THE DEAD
ARTFIRE FILMS
HTTP://WWW.MYSPACE.COM/DIARYOFTHEDEAD

'LIVING DEAD' SEQUELS

The enduring popularity of *Night of the Living Dead*, and the positive reception for *Dawn of the Dead*, ensured several more sequels, namely, *Day of the Dead, Land of the Dead*, and *Diary of the Dead*. The series charts different aspects of humanity's long-running battle with the forces of death, in the shape of the zombie apocalypse that threatens to drive the human race to extinction, and most of the films reference contemporary social and political issues from a critical standpoint.

DAY OF THE DEAD

In 1978, the co-writer of the script of *Night of the Living Dead*, John Russo, released a sequel entitled *Return of the Dead*, which continues the story set up in the original film. This provoked a bitter argument between Russo and Romero, since Romero saw *Return of the Dead* as a direct competitor to his own sequel, *Dawn of the Dead*, which was released in the same year. The conflict eventually was settled in court, and Russo was ordered to cease advertising his movie. As a result of this situation, Russo's film *Return of the Dead* is not generally regarded as the true sequel to *Night of the Living Dead*. However, *Return of the Dead* has spawned four more movies in the series, including two that have been released on television.

Day of the Dead, Land of the Dead, and *Diary of the Dead*, all by Romero, have in general received positive reviews, though there is some debate as to which is the strongest film. *Day of the Dead* was released in 1985, and was described by him as a 'tragedy about how a lack of human communication causes chaos and collapse even in this small little pie slice of society'. This theme had been present in his earlier movies, but now Romero explored it further, with mixed results.

Romero initially had high ambitions for the film, having received a total of US$7 million to make it. However, during the production process, this sum was cut to approximately half this amount, forcing him once more to use his resourcefulness in making striking films on a low budget. This he managed to do, despite all sorts of financial disputes, mechanical failures and other problems that arose during filming. (For example, since some of the scenes were shot underground, Romero used a mine shaft location, but the high humidity in the atmosphere made filming very difficult).

RAVAGED BY ZOMBIES

The plot of the movie concerns the zombie apocalypse portrayed in parts one and two of the Romero *Living Dead* movies, with a jump forward in time to a ravaged planet earth, where human survivors of the plague are few and far between. In an underground research station, a scientist, Doctor Logan, spends his time conducting gruesome experiments on zombies that he has captured, trying to find out more about them in an effort to understand how human beings and zombies can coexist in the future. The underground bunker is also inhabited by a guerilla leader, Rhodes, and his small band of followers. When a female scientist, Sarah, comes to the bunker to seek refuge, fighting breaks out between Logan and Rhodes, with catastrophic results.

The film contains extremely gory sequences, and so shocked the Unites States Conference of Catholic Bishops Office for Film and Broadcasting that it issued a statement saying, 'Director-writer George Romero's third low-budget zombie chilller provides a loathsome and unimaginative mix of violence, blood, gore and some sexual references demeaning to women'. Others, such as critic Janet Maslin, reviewing the film in the *New York Times*, complained that there was too much 'windy argument' in the movie. However, the female star of the film, Lori Cardillc, took issue with the idea that the film was sexist, and pointed out that her character, Sarah, was intelligent, strong and resourceful, rather than simply being depicted as a gun-toting sex symbol.

THE ZOMBIE MYTH: DIGGING DEEPER

Initially, reaction to *Day of the Dead* was not very positive, with many commentators suggesting that it was the weakest film in the series. It was seen as the most ambitious, yet least convincing, movie that Romero had made. Today, however, it is considered to be one of the most intriguing, if controversial, of his films. Although some believe the film features too much talk and not enough action, others find it more intellectually satisfying than the first two films, in that it tries to dig deeper into the zombie myth, asking what really drives these creatures from the grave. In addition, enthusiasts point to the special effects in the film, which are much more complex and impressively cxccutcd than in the first two of the *Living Dead* trilogy.

LAND OF THE DEAD

The next film to feature in the Romero series was *Land of the Dead*, released in 2005. During the 1990s, Romero did not release a zombie film, but in the new millennium, there was a spate of original zombie or zombie-related films, including *Resident Evil*, *28 Days Later* and *Shaun of the Dead* that encouraged him to make another movie. This movie, the fourth in the series, told the story of a zombie attack on the city of Pittsburgh, Pennsylvania, which, in his ongoing story, has now become like a medieval city, protected and fortified from the onslaught of the marauding hordes of zombies. The 'stenches', or zombies, so-called because of their rotting bodies, have become the main population of the planet, and have, worryingly, begun to show signs of increased intelligence.

STOMACH-TURNING SPECIAL EFFECTS

In a parody of modern urban society, the rich human survivors of the apocalypse live in a skyscraper, carefully guarded in their high-rise apartments, and separated off from the poor, who live miserable lives on the streets below. The rich community of the skyscraper hire a band of raiders to make occasional attacks on zombie strongholds to obtain food and other supplies. However, it seems that the zombies have now begun to remember skills from their past as living beings, and are not easily outwitted.

On its release, the film had positive reviews. A big budget extravaganza, it was generally considered to have delivered classy entertainment while still preserving Romero's trademark wit, irony and scathing social commentary. Critic Michael Wilmington wrote: 'It's another hard-edged, funny, playfully perverse and violent exercise in movie fear and loathing, with an increasingly dark take on a world spinning out of control. By now, Romero has become a classicist who uses character and dialogue as much as stomach-turning special effects to achieve his shivers'.

GORE AND POLITICS

In addition to the glossy production values, the film boasted a cast of stars, including Simon Baker, Dennis Hopper, John Leguizamo, and Asia Argento. Overall, *Land of the Dead* was seen as a successful transition on the part of its director, George Romero, from the low-budget 'cult' horror film to the mainstream blockbuster. Some saw in it a critique of the US response to the horrific events of 9/11, in which Bush and others effectively argued for an isolationist, vigilante position, presenting America as fighting singly-handedly against an 'axis of evil' – an unspecified foreign network of terror – and ignoring or denying US political involvement and support of regimes, such as in Saudi Arabia, that might have contributed to the outbreak of violence. Others preferred to view Romero's latest offering as pure entertainment, and were especially impressed by the special effects and make-up, seeing it as a horror film in the best comic-book tradition.

DIARY OF THE DEAD

Diary of the Dead, the next chapter in Romero's series of zombie films, premiered in 2007. The movie tells the story of a group of filmmakers who record the outbreak of a zombie attack, and inevitably become bound up in the violence themselves. It begins as a reporter stands in front of an ambulance, reporting on the murder of a family, who is then bitten by a supposed dead body being loaded into the vehicle. The action escalates, throughout the film, into a full-scale battle between the humans and the zombies.

In homage to some of his favourite writers, actors and film directors, the voices of Quentin Tarantino, Wes

Craven, Guillermo del Toro, Simon Pegg, and Stephen King were used as the newscasters on radio. Although reviews were mixed, the film was was, in general, positively received.

SURVIVAL OF THE DEAD

Romero's most recent film in the series is *Survival of the Dead*, which has been shown at film festivals but is currently still awaiting general release. Set only a few weeks after the initial outbreak of a zombie plague, the story follows some groups of survivors as they attempt to survive the latest episode in the apocalypse.

The film opens with a crisis scenario in which, worldwide, over fifty million people are dying each year, and then returning to feast on the living. The zombies, known as 'deadheads' take their sustenance from live human beings, who then become zombies themselves, *ad infinitum*.

TERRIBLE AFFLICTION

On a small island called Plum, off the coast of Delaware, two families of Irish extraction, the O'Flynns and the Muldoons, make matters more difficult for themselves by continuing their lifelong feud, this time disagreeing on how the zombies should be fought off. The leader of the O'Flynns wants to shoot them dead, even though many of them were previously members of their family. The leader of the Muldoons thinks that the zombies should be held captive and treated in a reasonably humane way until a cure for this terrible affliction can be found.

Matters reach crisis point when fighting breaks out between the two families. Meanwhile, a party of ruthless, rough and ready soldiers dedicated only to self-preservation arrive on the island, seeking a safe haven, and once there begin to rob, steal and fight in order to survive.

EXTREME CARNAGE

As in his other films, Romero manages to tuck some witty social and political commentary in amongst the gore. One critic, Ray Bennett, called it 'a polished, fast-moving entertaining picture whose mainstream success will depend on audiences' tolerance of its tendency to become an abattoir of extreme carnage.' For diehard zombie fans, there are ever more ingenious special effects, featuring exploding bodies and heads, with ghoulish make-up to match, and an array of revolting set pieces that will delight the most seasoned horror viewer.

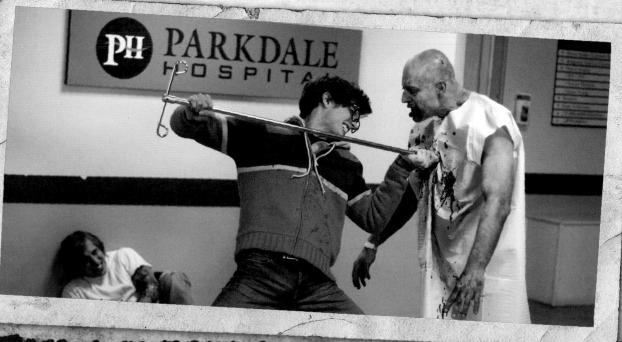

EVOLUTION OF THE HORROR ZOMBIE

On screen, the horror zombie has evolved – if that is the right way of putting it – quite dramatically since the 1930s, when it made its first appearance in the Halperin Brothers' *White Zombie*. The zombies set to work in the factory by the evil Murder Legendre are characterized by their stiff gait and staring eyes. They also have wooden expressions and seem to be emotionless. (Some harsh critics at the time also accused the principal actors of the drama as similarly handicapped.)

The 'white zombie' of the title, the beautiful young fiancé, Madeleine Short Parker, who is spirited away by Murder Legendre to be turned into a zombie for his nefarious, possibly sexual purposes, makes her first appearance after zombification looking pale and wan, with arms outstretched like a sleepwalker, dressed in nothing but a rather transparent negligee. On the poster advertising the film, Madeleine appears in this (lack of) garb under the legend, 'She was not alive nor dead, just a WHITE ZOMBIE … performing his every desire'. The titillating inference was that tremendous sexual adventures would occur, in which the female white zombie of the starring role would, in her half-dead state, be subjected to shocking sexual acts; however, no such excitements occurred in the film. Indeed, many years later, Victor Halperin appeared to regret the exploitative content of the film, remarking, 'I don't believe in fear, violence, and horror, so why traffic in them?'

Today, *White Zombie* is regarded by most film buffs as a remarkable movie, albeit with ambitions a little above the competence of the director and the cast. In particular, despite its far-fetched storyline and sometimes wooden acting (not just on the part of the zombies), it is admired for its brooding, threatening atmosphere. No doubt the presentation of the Caribbean voodoo legend, with Bela Lugosi as the sorceror, a cast of blank-eyed zombie factory workers, and the alluring Madge Bellamy as the young zombie bride, had much to do with creating this disturbing ambience. As one film historian remarked, 'Halperin shoots this poetic melodrama as trance… the

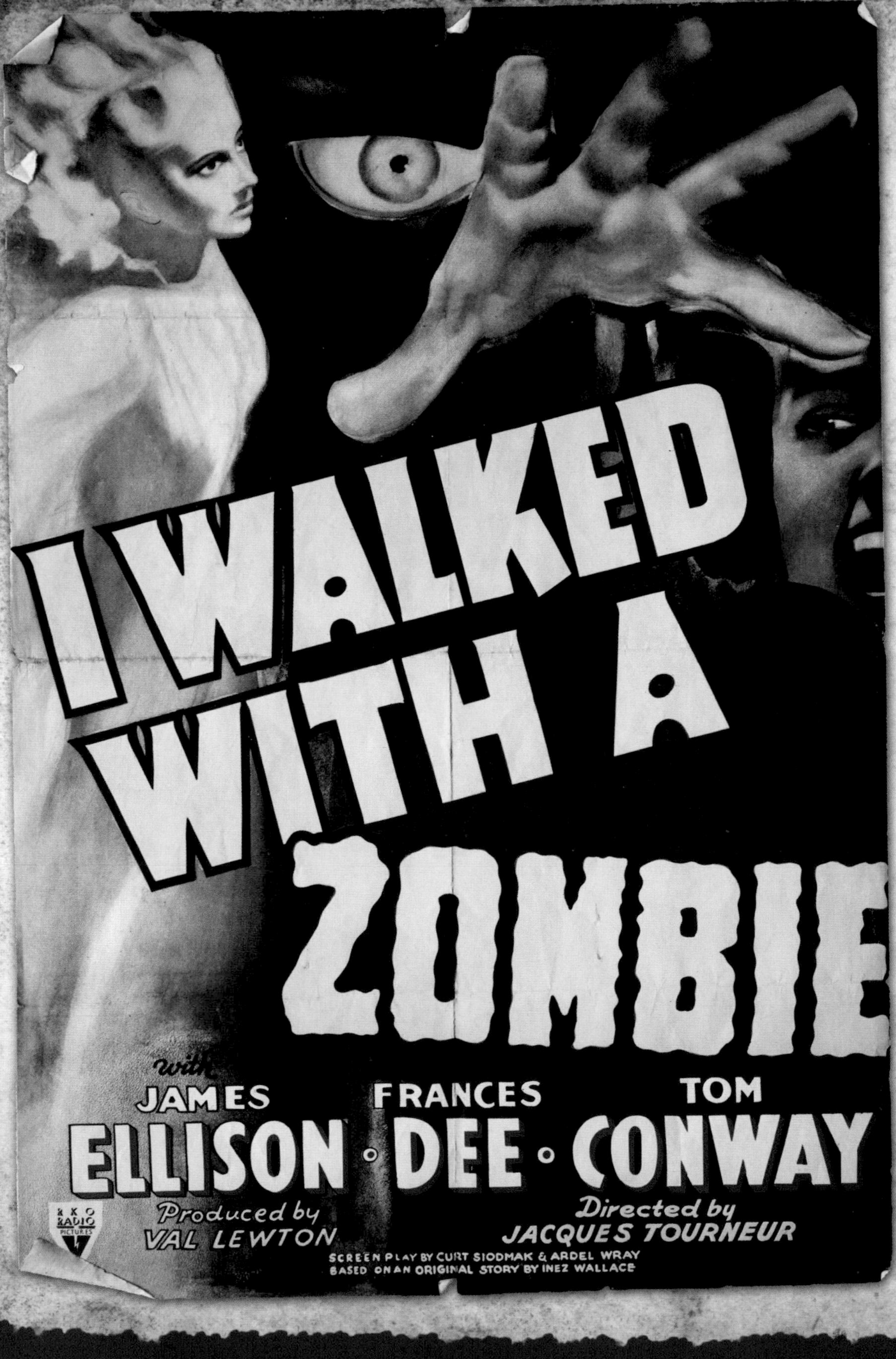

Above: Film poster for Jacques Tourneur's *I Walked with a Zombie*, 1943.

unique result constitutes a virtual bridge between classic Universal Horror and the later Val Lewton productions.'

I WALKED WITH A ZOMBIE

Val Lewton was a film producer for RKO pictures in the 1940s, who became known for a series of dark, menacing horror films throughout the decade. The second of these, *I Walked with a Zombie*, was directed by French-American Jacques Tourneur, and released in 1943. Lewton had worked with a group of writers to create the script, and used some ideas from *Jane Eyre* by Charlotte Brontë in the narrative. In keeping with his general cinematic style, Lewton blurred the distinction between reality and the supernatural, creating a strong tension between the two, and keeping his audiences guessing until the very end of the movie.

The zombie archetype was much more distinctly drawn in this film than in *White Zombie*, and there were various imaginative shots of zombies throughout. One of them consisted of a hugely tall, almost monstrous black man, with huge, staring eyes, and a blank expression on his face. In addition, there are many dream-like, poetic sequences that mimic the trance-like condition of the Caribbean voodoo zombie, with characters walking about at night as if in a dream. Thus, in this film, the horror zombie is very much akin to the voodoo zombie, taking its main features from the monstrous revenant, or 'undead' soul of West Indian myth and legend.

BRAIN FEVER

I Walked with a Zombie tells the story of a nurse named Betsy who goes for an interview as a private caregiver. During the interview, she is closely questioned as to her opinions on witchcraft, for reasons that we find out about later. She gets the job, persuaded into it by talk of palm trees and sunshine, and travels to the West Indies to take up her position. Arriving on the unspoiled island, she is initially enchanted by the beautiful scenery. However, her new employer, Paul Holland, turns out to be a rather morbid character, constantly talking about death and disaster. His coach driver is a similarly lugubrious soul, and Betsy soon realises that, though sunny, her new environment is far from happy.

Taking his cue from Charlotte Brontë's tale of the madwoman in the attic, Lewton then has Betsy wake up in the middle of the night, hearing an eerie scream. She then meets her new charge, Jessica Holland, walking along in a nightdress, staring sightlessly in front of her. She is terrified, and screams for help. The next day, Paul explains that the cry she heard comes from the African slaves on the island, who 'still weep when a child is born – and make merry at a burial'. Betsy also meets Jessica's doctor, a man named Maxwell, who tells her that Jessica's illness has been caused by an incurable tropical fever affecting the spine and the brain.

CROSSROADS ZOMBIE MONSTER

Later in the story, Betsy learns from a calypso singer (played by the renowned Sir Lancelot, a singer and actor who influenced Harry Belafonte) that Jessica's condition is the result of a shock suffered since she fell in love with another man, Wesley Rand, and tried to elope with him. Betsy returns to the mansion, determined to restore Jessica to health, and tries to bring her back to normality by administering insulin, but to no avail. Jessica's maid, Alma, then tells Betsy that there is one way

to cure their mistress: through the incantations of a voodoo priest who lives on the island. Betsy resolves to take Jessica to see the priest, hoping that he will be able to help her.

In a highly atmospheric sequence, Betsy and Jessica steal out at night, walking through the cane fields. On the way, they encounter strange animal sacrifices hanging from the trees and the monstrous zombie who guards the crossroads. Eventually, they come to the priest's village and watch as the villagers gather for the ceremony. Here the plot begins to be rather far-fetched, as it turns

ABOVE: Scene still from *I Walked With a Zombie*, Jacques Tourneur, 1943.

out that the priest is none other than Mrs Rand, Paul's mother, who also just happens to be a medical doctor. Mrs Rand explains, not very convincingly, that she pretends to use voodoo magic so that the native people will come to accept standard Western medicine. She tells Betsy that it is no use trying to cure Jessica, as her condition is incurable. Meanwhile, the villagers' curiosity is aroused by Jessica's zombie-like trance. They perform a test on her, using a sword, and are satisfied that she is a zombie who does not have any warm blood in her body.

VOODOO SPELL

Next, Betsy finds herself falling in love with Paul, despite his miserable outlook and dreary observations on life. Meanwhile, an investigation is being carried out into the cause of Jessica's malaise, during which Mrs Rand reveals that, after discovering Jessica and Wesley's secret liaison, and their plan to elope together, she put a voodoo spell on her daughter-in-law that turned her into a zombie. In the final denouement, the two lovers jump into the sea, pursued by the monster crossroads zombie, and are drowned, leaving Paul and Betsy free to pursue their romance.

Despite the weaknesses of the film in terms of plot, there were many who admired its sensitive handling of the zombie myth, and its intelligent approach to the ethnic culture of the voodoo religion. In addition, the black characters in the film were portrayed sympathetically. As with many of Val Lewton's movies, the boundary between reality and the supernatural was explored in an

ambiguous way: we never discover whether Jessica truly is a zombie, or whether the villagers' beliefs have any basis in fact.

I Walked with a Zombie proved, in later years, to be a popular movie with horror fans, and the title also made an entry into psychedelic rock in a song by Rocky Erikson (see page 175-6).

PAPA LEGBA

The zombie monster at the crossroads in *I Walked with a Zombie* was modelled on the voodoo god or loa Papa Legba. In the voodoo religion, the spirit of Papa Legba often shows himself as a demon at the crossroads, most often in a remote area. He is envisioned as a young, lusty man whose skin is red and who drinks rum spiced with gunpowder. Since this spirit guards the crossroads, it is he who decides who can travel up and down the roads, according to his own laws. In some versions of the myth, he is closely identified with Satan; in others, he is merely inclined to mischief, and to allowing misfortunes of different kinds to happen to travellers who pass his way.

As in *White Zombie*, the main zombie character in *I Walked with a Zombie* is a young, pretty white woman wearing a diaphanous white dress. In one of the posters advertising the film, the woman is depicted as being carried in the arms of a very tall, well-built black man. She appears to have fainted. The line above reads, 'The blackest magic of voodoo keeps this woman alive... yet dead!' (see page 165). Once again, the poster emphasises the sensationalist aspects of the film, with the comatose white woman appearing to be carried off by a large black man, suggesting all manner of evil intentions on his part; however, in the actual film, this is not the case and the zombie of the title is the woman herself. The imposing black figure is the loa who guards the crossroads, also conceived of as a zombie in the movie.

BAD ZOMBIE MOVIES OF THE FIFTIES

During the 1950s, zombie horror movies continued to be made, but they were few and far between. It was not until a decade later that this section of the horror market became a recognisable genre. Moreover, the zombie movies made in this period were not considered to be great works of art, to say the least. One of them was *Teenage Zombies*, written and directed by Jerry Warren, and released in 1959. This tells the story of a group of teenage friends who go on a boating trip and discover an island run by a mad scientist intent on zombifying the population of the US. After many adventures, most of them extremely unlikely, there is a final fight involving a de-zombified gorilla who saves them from the clutches of the insane Doctor Myra. The zombies in this film are much like the 'voodoo horror' zombies of the forties, in that they move stiffly and appear to be in a trance-like state. *Teenage Zombies* is generally considered today to be a less than great film, using stock footage from other films by Jerry Warren. Later, the title was used for a video game called *Teenage Zombies: The Invasion of the Alien Brain Thingys*.

BELA LUGOSI: THE UNDEAD RISES AGAIN?

Another substandard movie of the period was entitled *Plan 9 from Outer Space*, also released in 1959. Originally known as *Grave Robbers from Outer Space*, it proved to be as lurid and ridiculous as the title suggests. Written by Edward D. Wood Jnr, it supposedly starred Bela Lugosi, although he had died three years earlier. (He was not resurrected as a zombie, but the director had shot footage of him before he died for another movie, and cobbled it into this film, with continuity results that were at worst incompetent, and at best, hilarious.) In the film, extraterrestrial beings concoct a plan to conquer the earth by resurrecting the dead as zombies and allowing them to invade unnoticed. The film received very little attention on its release, and in the years that followed, was occasionally shown on TV, until in 1980, when critic Michael Medved declared it to be 'the worst movie ever made'. Many would agree, though some commentators have pointed out that the film's gaffs make it highly entertaining, and therefore not tedious or dull, as a truly bad movie should be.

PLAGUE OF THE ZOMBIES

In 1966, the British Hammer Horror studios released *The Plague of the Zombies*, directed by John Gilling. At the heart of the film was the image of the mindless, shuffling zombie as a revenant from the grave, as seem in the films of the 1940s and 1950s, but in this horror movie, the monsters

become much more grotesque. They are cadavers from freshly dug graves, still rotting, and as such they prefigure the gory zombies of George Romero's lurid imagination in *Night of the Living Dead*.

The film begins as a scientist, Sir James Forbes, and his daughter Sylvia, travel to a remote Cornish village to visit a former student, Peter Tompson. There he finds Peter's wife Alice in a strange, trance-like condition, and hears Peter tell of a mysterious plague that has affected the villagers. It soon transpires that the village is in the grip of a zombie plague, and Sylvia witnesses Alice being carried off in the arms of a cadaverous man that she had earlier seen lying dead in a coffin. The group find out that a local squire, Clive Hamilton, who previously lived for many years in the Caribbean, has been raising the dead. Many adventures ensue, and the action takes place in the kind of atmosphere that the Hammer films evoked so well: shrouded mists, remote moorlands and eerie old houses.

Today, the film is seen as a bridge between the voodoo zombie depicted in films such as *White Zombie* and *I Walked with a Zombie*, in that it makes reference to the traditional Caribbean zombie while introducing a new image of it into the horror genre: that of the gore-covered, rotting undead corpse, fresh from its sojourn in the grave. However, in *Plague of the Zombies*, the zombies have not, as yet, taken to eating live human beings. Nor do they suffer from a desire to drink warm blood and eat brains. At this stage of their cinematic evolution, all they want

is to throttle human beings and, apparently, cause as much fear and mayhem as possible for the purposes of audience entertainment.

Gilling's zombies are, characteristically, dressed in their burial shrouds, looking like medieval monks. Inside these dark hoods, their glassy eyes burn malevolently. In a striking twilight shot, the first zombie appears at the mouth of an old tin mine, in another, the doctor looks on as the dead rise from the graveyard, which is lit with a green hue. This aspect of the film may have influenced director Lucio Fulci in his seventies movie *Zombie Flesh Eaters* (1979), since there is a remarkably similar shot in the later film.

THE BRAIN-MUNCHING ZOMBIE

Some horror zombie fanatics, when referring to the history of the genre on screen, refer to 'BR' and 'AR', meaning, before and after George Romero, the director of *Night of the Living Dead*, which started a new craze for the zombie movie . As mentioned on page 122, the zombie of Romero's imagination was a new, though not necessarily improved creature who differed greatly from the zombie of earlier films. In particular, the Romero zombie had a grotesque visual impact, being covered in gore, with a distinctive pallor and stiff, lumbering gait.

Shot in black and white, *Night of the Living Dead* showed zombies dressed in ordinary street or work clothes, or in sleepwear, which stressed the point that zombification was a contemporary plague that could affect ordinary people, sometimes interrupting their lives quite suddenly, and sending them into an eternal half-life, or undead condition, wandering the earth in search of sustenance in the shape of warm human brains and blood. The classic line of the film, 'They're coming to get you, Barbra' epitomised the jokey, yet seriously frightening, quality of the film: as Johnny, Barbra's brother taunts her, a 'real' zombie emerges from the graveyard to carry her off.

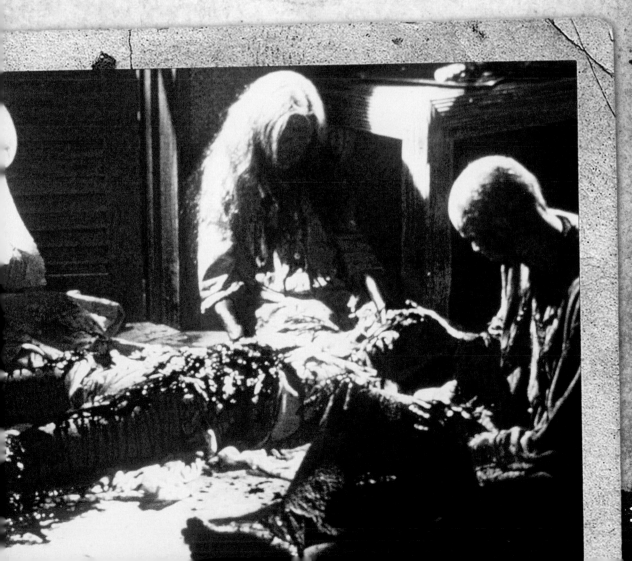

EVOLUTION OF THE HORROR ZOMBIE II: THE SEVENTIES & BEYOND

In the seventies, the evolution of the horror zombie continued apace with an eclectic mixture of films including *Tombs of the Blind Dead* (1971), *Children Shouldn't Play with Dead Things, Garden of the Dead* (both 1972), *Horror Rises from the Tomb* (1973), and *Night of the Seagulls* (1975). In 1978, Romero once again made horror history with his seminal *Dawn of the Dead*, presaging the gruesome gore fest that was to characterize the screen zombie from that point on.

ZOMBI 2

A year later, an Italian film director named Lucio Fulci released *Zombi 2*, another gory epic. Fulci's zombies were shown smothered from head to toe in blood, chained to railings as though they had pulled themselves free, and with hideous grey faces. Many felt that Fulci was copying Romero, but as it transpired, he had been making the film at the same time as *Dawn of the Dead*, so this was not the case. Fulci entitled his film *Zombi 2* so that it would not be mixed up with *Dawn of the Dead*, which was known as *Zombi* in some countries. Rather confusingly, *Zombi 2* is also known as *Zombie Flesh Eaters*.

By the end of the seventies, the fully-fledged zombie cadaver, complete with rotting flesh, lumbering gait and hideous, pallid face had come into being. In the years that followed, zombies began to take over the world – on screen at least – and found their way into Chinese and Asian films, particularly martial arts movies. In these, zombies are often depicted as beings in a trance-like state who are suddenly animated by a magician, and prove to be fearsome fighters. Today, the zombie as villain is still a feature of many martial arts movies, but the horror zombie film as a genre has not proved as popular as in the West.

THE EVIL DEAD

In the eighties, the zombie horror flick gained in popularity, and many more films were made, such as *Hell of the Living Dead* (1981), and *Return of the Living Dead* (1985). *Return of the Living Dead*, directed by Dan O'Bannon, introduced a strong comedy element into the genre, telling the story of a group of teenagers fighting a horde of zombies, saving their town from the apocalypse. The film was notable for featuring zombies who lust after human brains rather than simply human flesh; their cry of 'Brains!' amused and shocked their viewers, and became part of zombie vocabulary from then on. The film also became successful because of its soundtrack, which featured various punk rock bands that were popular at that time.

In 1981 came *The Evil Dead*, which did a great deal to establish the zombie movie as a staple of the horror genre. The film tells the story of people possessed by evil spirits, who then become zombies. Their faces develop a white crust over them, and their eyes become white, with black circles around them. Written and directed by Sam Raimi, the film followed the adventures of five college students who take a holiday in a cabin in a remote forest, and then find an audiotape which

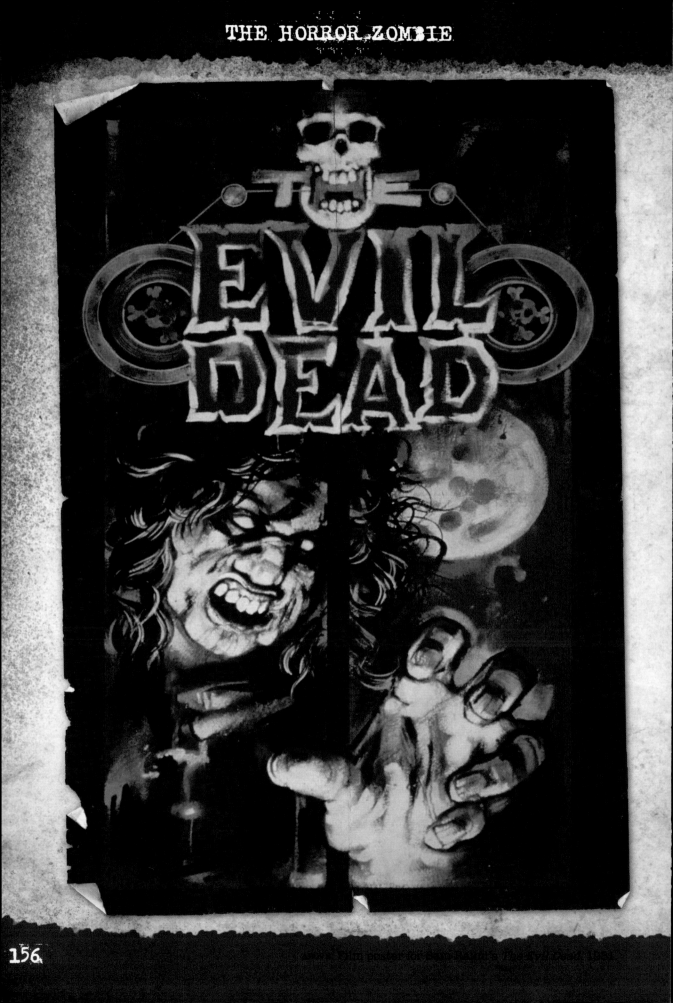

A horror film poster for Sam Raimi's The Evil Dead, 1981.

releases evil spirits. The film, also known as *The Book of the Dead*, and *The Evil Dead, the Ultimate Experience in Grueling Horror* was extremely violent and gory, and for a long time was not able to find a distributor in the US. Although it had been made on a low budget, it did reasonably well at the box office, and gained a loyal following of fans. Since then, there have been two sequels, *Evil Dead II* and *Army of Darkness*.

ZOMBIES IN OVERDRIVE

From this point on, the zombie horror movie went into overdrive, with a tremendous rise in the number of films made. Not all of them were memorable by any means, but they came thick and fast, and among them were some durable successes, notably: *Dead and Buried* (1981), *Zombie Island Massacre* (1984), *Day of the Dead* (1985), *Night of the Creeps* (1986), and *The Dead Next Door* (1988). In addition, films like *Re-Animator* (1985), *Creepshow* (1985), *The Serpent and the Rainbow* (1988) and *Waxwork* (1988) introduced new audiences to the burgeoning screen cult of the horror zombie.

During this period, a number of important rules regarding zombies were established in the genre. Firstly, it became clear that all zombies must die first – in some films up to this point, the zombies were merely in a trance; secondly, that they must not feed on each other, like cannibals, but only on human flesh, especially their favourite delicacy, warm brains; thirdly, that they may only be killed by a gunshot to the head (other ways of killing them, such as using a knife, an ice pick, a gun, and so on, will not be effective); and finally, that zombies are not very intelligent. This last characteristic was particularly important, since it gave the movies an opportunity to present an epic struggle between 'brains' and 'brawn' – the intelligence of live human beings, who may be able to outwit the zombies if they use their brains, versus the lumbering strength of the slow-witted yet vicious undead.

BUB: THE SYMPATHETIC ZOMBIE

The zombies of the eighties were, if anything, even more gory than their predecessors, sometimes – as in *The Dead Next Door* – trailing broken chains and wearing masks that are intended to stop them biting human beings. In some cases, certain zombies show levels of intelligence – for example Bub, the pet zombie from *Day of the Dead*, who listens to a walkman. Bub is also notable for introducing the idea that zombies can be, to a certain extent, sympathetic characters. Bub echoes Mary Shelley's *Frankenstein* in that, dangerous and strong as he is, we feel sorry for him and pity his condition. Unlike most zombies, Bub appears to have a personality and a soul, and to find his situation painful and difficult. As some critics have remarked, in this film, Romero portrays Bub, the domesticated zombie, as somewhat more likeable than his human captors.

DEAD ALIVE (BRAINDEAD)

Zombie film-making continued apace in the nineties, with an avalanche of new zombie films, most of which were less than original. However, there were some classics of the genre, including *Dead Alive* (1992) and *Cemetery Man* (1994).

Braindead (released in the US as *Dead Alive*) is a comedy horror directed by Peter Jackson, who later went on to direct the *Lord of the Rings* trilogy. It concerns an exotic rat-monkey which infects human beings by biting them, turning them into ravenous zombies. The film tells the story of a man whose mother becomes one of these zombies, and his horrifying but sometimes comical efforts to deal with the situation. As hordes of zombies begin to take over the world, he finally confronts his monstrous mother, who tries to stuff him into her womb, but he cuts his way out. Due to the extreme nature of the gore in the film, many versions of it were censored, but over time it has become a cult classic.

DELLAMORTE DELLAMORE (CEMETERY MAN)

Another outstanding film from the period is *Dellamorte Dellamore*, also known as *Cemetery Man*, directed by Michele Soavi and based on a novel by Tiziano Sclavi. Starring Rupert Everett, the narrative tells of a cemetery caretaker in a small

THE HORROR ZOMBIE *Dead Alive* (*Braindead*), Peter Jackson, 1992

Italian town. Francesco Dellamorte, the caretaker, has a handicapped son, and his job involves destroying revenants from the grave, who keep rising up and threatening to overrun the town. Thus, in a parody of the work life of ordinary folk, with their soulless round of dull tasks, Francesco and his son are forced to spend their time shooting zombies to prevent a major outbreak of zombie plague. When at last Francesco falls in love, the situation worsens, until he is reduced to the same level of imbecility as his son.

On its release in Italy, the film made little impact, but later found a cult following in the US. Director Martin Scorsese called it one of the best films to come out of Italy during the 1990s. However, among zombie horror fans, there is some controversy as to whether it is a true zombie horror, and indeed, it does break the genre rules, being a mixture of horror, comedy and romance, with a strong philosophical undertow, and prefiguring later movies such as *Donnie Darko*.

THE 'ZOM COMS'

As well as the horror elements of the zombie movie, there has always been a comic thread underlying the graphic representations of gore and violence. In the same way that medical students make sick jokes about the human body, operations, and so on, zombie film makers are very much inclined to present the funnier aspects of decomposition and mutilation of the human body, perhaps as a way of relieving the truly horrific aspects of death and destruction.

Thus, in the evolution of the zombie myth, there have been a number of movies that have emphasised the humour involved in this enduring legend. As early as 1949 we find the character Bombie the Zombie in Disney comic books. As we have noted, comedy runs through many of Romero's films, and is a central motif in films such as *Return of the Living Dead* and *Dellamorte Delamore*. In the nineties, films such as *My Boyfriend's Back* continued this theme in a lighter vein, telling the story of a teenage boy who comes back from the dead to keep a date with his girlfriend.

In the new millennium, films such as *Fido* (2006), directed by Andrew Currie, which takes place in a parallel universe where space radiation has turned the dead into zombies, and *Zombie Strippers* (2008), about a group of strippers who bite their customers and turn them into zombies, have explored this thread of surreal humour with entertaining results. But perhaps more significantly, the genre zombie films themselves, while presenting the lust, violence and gore of the zombie myth in all its horror, have often been able to make tongue-in-cheek observations at the same time. The best of them, such as Romero's films, have also given us serious food for thought with wry political and social commentary that has remained topical and relevant in the new century.

ZOMBIES OF THE NEW MILLENNIUM

In the new millennium, an enormous number of zombie films continue to be released. However, very few of them merit serious consideration, relying mostly on gore and special effects to appeal to an adolescent or young male audience. But there are some that have become cult classics, with good reason, since they are witty and entertaining, as well as providing a good, old-fashioned slice of zombie mayhem for up-and-coming generations of zombie lovers to enjoy. The British film *28 Days Later* (2002), while not strictly a zombie horror movie, nevertheless mined a similar territory to Matheson's *I Am Legend* (see page 108), which in turn inspired the films of George Romero. In an extremely well realised, imaginative scenario of post-apocalyptic London, it tells the story of the breakdown of civilisation, caused by a virus that infects the population. Directed by Danny Boyle, it was very positively received, both by critics and audiences.

SHAUN OF THE DEAD

A more light-hearted approach to the subject of death and destruction was presented in another British film, *Shaun of the Dead*, which was released in 2004. Directed by Edgar Wright, it tells the story of a man with a host of personal and familial

ABOVE: Scene still from *Shaun of the Dead*, Edgar Wright, 2004.

difficulties, who then finds himself embroiled in fighting a zombie uprising.

The plot centres around a salesman, Shaun, who spends most of his time in the pub with his friends, to the dissatisfaction of his girlfriend, Liz, who finally dumps him. He resolves to win her back, and begins his quest by involving himself in resisting a zombie uprising in London. When his friend Pete becomes a zombie, Shaun realizes that he must act, and rounds up his friends, including his former girlfriend, to sit out the attack in the pub. After many adventures, the group barricade themselves into the pub, and begin to confess their secrets to each other.

THE RISE OF THE 'ZOM ROM COM'

When the zombies break in, Shaun is forced to shoot his mother, who has been bitten in the fight. This is the occasion of much hilarity in the film. Some of the group perish, while others survive. Eventually, Shaun and Liz manage to escape, with the help of another friend.

Critics mostly loved the film, as did audiences. One critic called it, 'a side-splitting, head smashing, gloriously gory horror comedy', while another commented that the script was 'crammed with real gags'. In addition, novelist Stephen King gave it a score of ten 'on the fun meter' and predicted that it would become a cult classic. George Romero asked the director, Edgar Wright, and the lead actor, Simon Pegg, to take cameo roles in one of his films, but instead they opted to be zombies, in each case fulfilling a lifelong ambition.

Today, *Shaun of the Dead* is classed as one of the best horror comedy films of all time, and is considered to be the first in a new genre, that of the 'zom rom com' (the zombie romantic comedy). Yet as well as being a very contemporary film, it also harks back to the early days of the zombie legend, with its critique of the alienation and soulless quality of modern life.

The publicity poster for the film shows an overcrowded tube train (typical of London's overstretched, underground system) with grey faces of passengers squashed against the glass, their eyes white, and expressions of misery, boredom, and pain etched on their faces. Among the passengers is a man with a worried expression on his face (the Shaun of the title) and a brightly coloured bunch of flowers, symbolising the attempt to find love and vitality in a colourless, deadened world. 'Ever felt you were surrounded by zombies?' reads the copy line, an apt question for anyone who has ever remarked on the strangely unfriendly, inhuman behaviour people tend to adopt on underground travel systems.

As with zombie films of previous decades, the film attempts to deal with the problem of how to find meaning and direction in modern life, and, in a light-hearted solution, suggests engaging in the battle to save civilisation from its deathly march towards uniformity and dullness – not to mention zombies covered in gore.

TOP ZOMBIE MOVIES

WHITE ZOMBIE

Director Victor Halperin (1932). Starring Bela Lugosi, Madge Bellamy, Robert W. Frazer.

A young woman is turned into a zombie (by Bela Lugosi) in Haiti, so local cad Charles Beamont can have his way with her. But now she seems a little pale and wan... *White Zombie* was the original zombie movie and it set the bar – low – with wooden acting and bad reviews. Today, critics are slightly more forgiving of the movie where it all began regarding it as a minor classic of the genre.

I WALKED WITH A ZOMBIE

Director Jacques Tourneur (1943). Starring Frances Dee, Christine Gordon, Tom Conway.

A nurse travels to the Caribbean to look after a plantation manager's wife, who seems, by all accounts, to be a zombie. Suspecting Voodoo the nurse turns to the local priests, but events take an unexpected turn (or three). Following *White Zombie*, *I Walked* focuses more on the myth of Voodoo in the Caribbean, than zombies and the undead.

NIGHT OF THE LIVING DEAD

Director George A. Romero (1968). Starring Duane Jones, Judith O'Dea, Karl Harman.

Seven people hole themselves up in a Pennsylvania farmhouse to escape a horde of hungry, incessant, lumbering zombies, who can only be killed by a blow to the head. Romero's first foray into zombie flicks not only revolutionised the genre and invented splatter movies, but also created the first 'edible' on screen human body, made from Bosco Chocolate Sauce and ham.

LET SLEEPING CORPSES LIE

Director Jorge Grau (1974). Starring Ray Lovelock, Arthur Kennedy, Cristina Galbó.

A young couple is suspected of murder while visiting the countryside. In fact, responsibility lies with the undead, who have been reanimated by a radiation-emitting device designed to kill insects. Since actor Fernando Hilbeck's zombie was meant to have died drowning, director Jorge Grau kept him soaked with water throughout filming. Grau said this often annoyed Hilbeck.

SHOCK WAVES

Director Ken Wiederhorn (1977). Starring Peter Cushing, Brooke Adams, John Carradine.

A yacht runs aground on an isolated island inhabited by an ageing SS Officer, who had once commanded a submarine crew of zombie Nazis. But hold on, what's that rising up from the depths? The original zombie Nazi

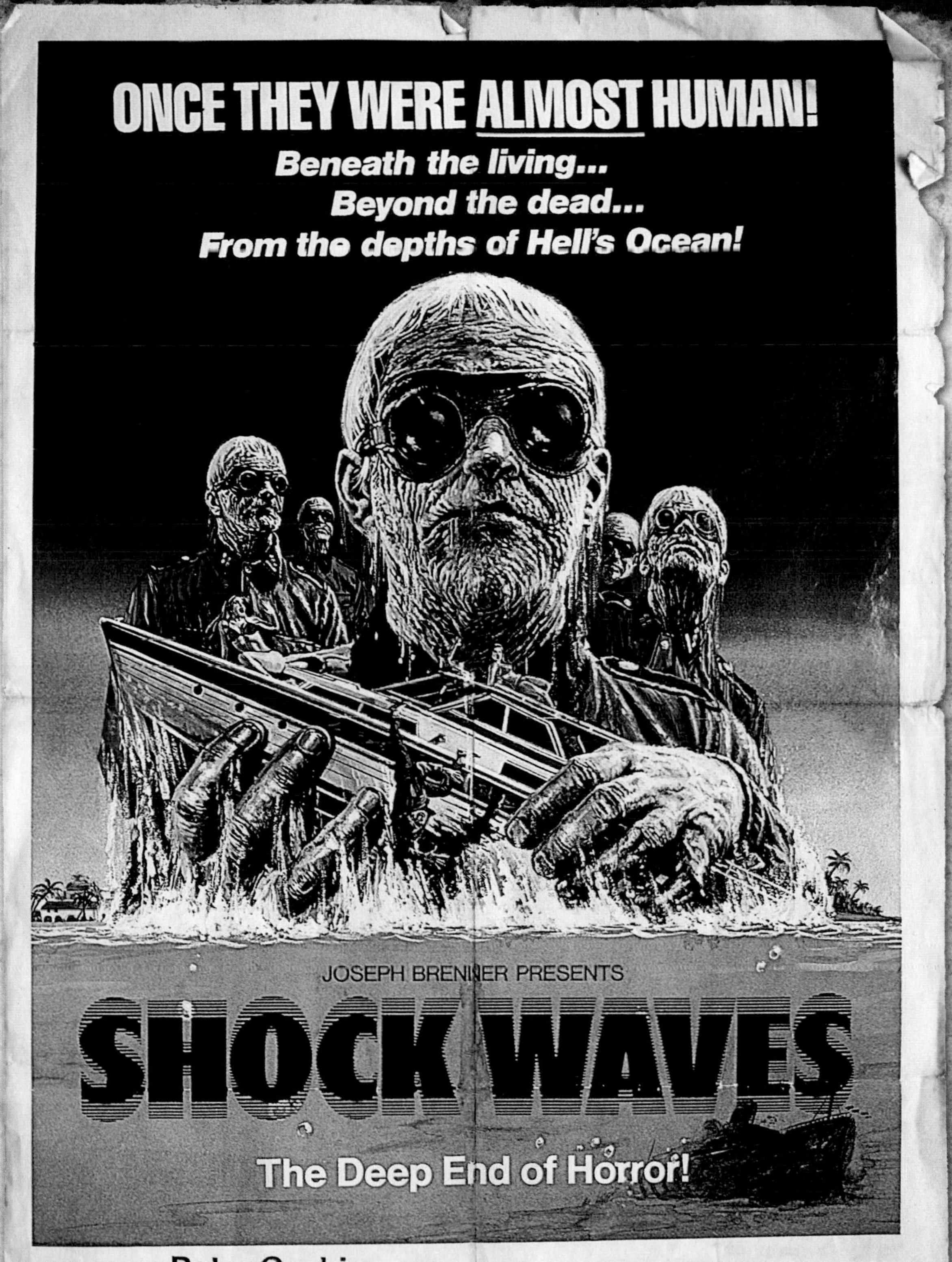

ABOVE: Film poster for Ken Wiederhorn's *Shock Waves*, 1977

When there's
no more room in HELL
the dead will walk the EARTH
First there was
'NIGHT OF THE
LIVING DEAD'
Now
GEORGE A.
ROMERO'S
DAWN
OF THE
DEAD
HERBERT R. STEINMANN & BILLY BAXTER PRESENT A LAUREL GROUP PRODUCTION in Association with CLAUDIO ARGENTO & ALFREDO CUOMO
Starring: DAVID EMGE KEN FOREE SCOTT H. REINIGER GAYLEN ROSS
Director of Photography: MICHAEL GORNICK Music By: THE GOBLINS with DARIO ARGENTO
Produced By: RICHARD P. RUBINSTEIN Written and Directed by: GEORGE A. ROMERO
READ THE ST. MARTIN'S BOOK TECHNICOLOR® ©DAWN ASSOCIATES MCMLXXVIII Released by UNITED FILM DISTRIBUTION CO.
There is no explicit sex in this picture.
However, there are scenes of violence which may be considered shocking.
No one under 17 will be admitted.

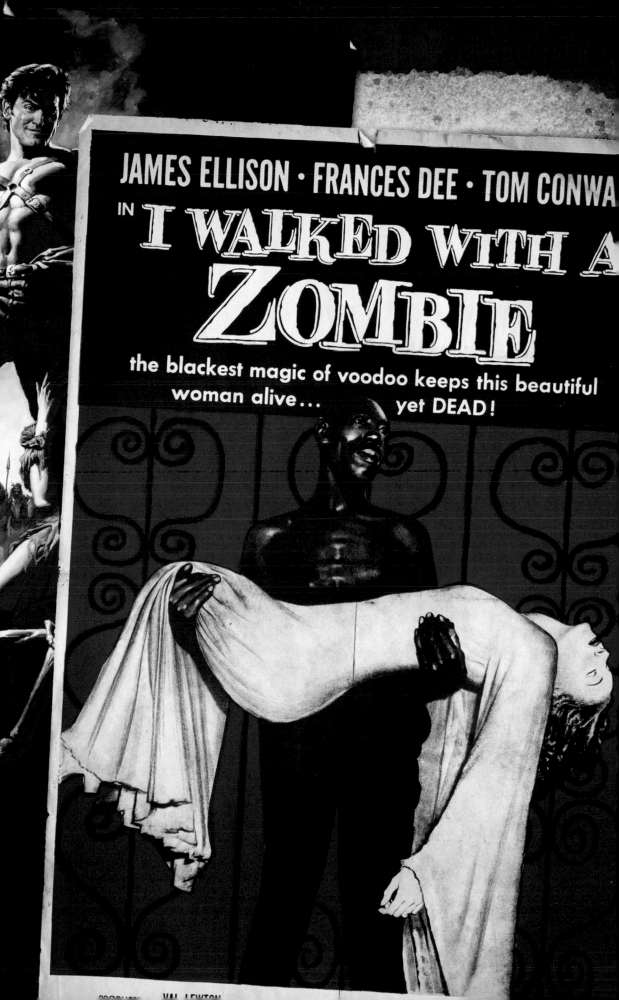

ABOVE: Scene still from *Return of the Living Dead*, Dan O'Bannon, 1985.

movie was filmed over 35 days in a dilapidated Florida hotel, which cost £250 to rent for the whole shoot.

DAWN OF THE LIVING DEAD

Director George A. Romero (1978). Starring David Emge, Ken Foree, Scott H. Reiniger.
It is a few weeks after *Night of the Living Dead* and a group hole themselves up in a deserted shopping mall. But just outside militant bikers and the undead roam the streets. Slated by the Catholic Church but loved by moviegoers, *Dawn* was the most profitable of the Living Dead series, bringing in $55 million from a production budget of $650,000.

ZOMBI 2

Director Lucio Fulci (1979). Starring Tisa Farrow, Ian McCulloch, Al Cliver.
A woman travels to a Caribbean island in search of her missing father. There, she finds a doctor trying to cure a zombie outbreak. 'Barf bags' were handed out to *Zombi 2* moviegoers because of the high level of gore and violence, which included a fight between a zombie and real-life tiger shark.

RETURN OF THE LIVING DEAD

Director Dan O'Bannon (1985). Starring Clu Gulager, James Karen, Don Calfa.
A deadly gas is released from a medical supply warehouse that reanimates the dead and sends them hunting for 'Braaaains'. Luckily some teenage misfits are on the case, spurred on by an 1980s punk rock soundtrack. Based on a John Russo (co-writer of *Night of the Living Dead*) novel, *Return* introduced slapstick, one-liners and nudity to the genre.

RE-ANIMATOR

Director Stuart Gordon (1985). Starring Jeffrey Combs, Bruce Abbott, Barbara Crampton.
A medical student conduct experiments on reanimating the dead. Not content with bringing back cats, he breaks into a hospital morgue to find some cadavers – with predictable results. Ground beef, cow by-products and 25 gallons of blood were used in this camp but gory rendition of H. P. Lovecraft's Herbert West: Reanimator.

DAY OF THE LIVING DEAD

Director George A. Romero (1985). Starring Lori Cardille, Terry Alexander, Joe Pilato.
In this sequel to *Dawn of the Dead* zombies rule the USA except for a few soldiers and scientists carrying out gruesome experiments on the undead in their bunker. Romero paid his zombie extras from the film's climax with a I Played a Zombie in 'Day of the Dead' cap, a newspaper headlined 'THE DEAD WALK', and one dollar.

EVIL DEAD 2

Director Sam Raimi (1987). Starring Bruce Campbell, Sarah Berry.
Ash, the sole survivor of *The Evil Dead*, returns to the cursed cabin in the woods where his girlfriend becomes a zombie, his hand becomes

possessed, and it is promised that Ash will be 'Dead by dawn!' Stephen King liked the comedy/horror *Evil Dead* so much he convinced producer Dino De Laurentiis to finance the sequel, which was mostly shot inside a high school gymnasium.

DEAD ALIVE (BRAINDEAD)

Director Peter Jackson (1992). Starring Timothy Balme, Elizabeth Moody, Diana Peñalver.
An infected Sumatran rat-monkey is shipped to a New Zealand zoo where it bites the hero's mother and unleashes a zombie-plague on 1950s Wellington. Split between romance, comedy and carnage, Braindead was heavily cut for the US and German markets to reduce the zombie-death-by-lawnmower scene. The third of director Jackson's horror/splatter movies, predates *Lord of the Rings* and *King Kong*.

ARMY OF DARKNESS

Director Sam Raimi (1993). Starring Bruce Campbell, Embeth Davidtz. In this sequel to *Evil Dead 2* Ash is transported back to medieval times with his car, shotgun and chainsaw. He has to find the Necronomicon book to return home, but instead unleashes the skeletal Army of Darkness. It has become a cult classic.

DELLAMORTE DELLAMORE (CEMETERY MAN)

Director Michele Soavi (1994).
Rupert Everett, François Hadji-Lazaro, Anna Falchi.
A caretaker of an Italian cemetery searches for love, while destroying the zombies that are unexpectedly rising from their graves. The sets for this romantic zombie comedy were built on real Italian cemeteries and the crew reported 'ghostly goings-on' when they removed some bones during filming.

VERSUS

Director Ryuhei Kitamura (2000).
Starring Tak Sakaguchi, Hideo Sakaki, Chieko Misaka.
A gangster is shot in a standoff on a remote forest road. But then he comes back to life, as do the other victims killed and buried there by the gangsters. Now there are scores to settle. Over 75 per cent of this Japanese film was reworked in 2004 for its DVD release to feature new scenes, new music and more blood.

28 DAYS LATER

Director Danny Boyle (2002). Starring Cillian Murphy, Naomie Harris, Brendan Gleeson.

Animal rights' activists accidently release the 'Rage' virus upon the United Kingdom resulting in the destruction of society. Twenty-eight days later courier Jim wakes up to find London almost deserted, apart for some very angry infected. Purists dismissed *28* because the zombies are not the undead, but the result of a blood-borne virus; and they can run instead of the traditional 'Romero-eqse' zombie stagger.

RESIDENT EVIL

Director Paul W.S Anderson (2002) Starring Mila Jovovich.

Based on the mega-successful computer games *Resident Evil 1* and *Resident Evil 2* (see below) the film follows heroine Alice and a platoon of commandos trying to escape a secret underground complex overrun with pursuing zombies. The film was commercially successful spawning three equally successful sequels *Resident Evil:Apocalypse* (2004), *Resident Evil:Extinction* (2007) and *Resident Evil:Afterlife* (2010).

Above: Scene still from *Planet Terror* (part of the Grindhouse double feature), Robert Rodriguez, 2007.

SHAUN OF THE DEAD

Director Edgar Wright (2004). Starring Simon Pegg, Nick Frost, Dylan Moran.

Dumped by his girlfriend and stuck in a dead-end existence, Shaun attempts to saved his loved ones from a zombie-apocalypse, armed only with a cricket bat and his useless best friend. After watching comedy/horror *Shaun of the Dead* zombie godfather George A. Romero offered Pegg and Wright roles in his *Land of The Dead* – they insisted on playing zombies.

PLANET TERROR

Director Robert Rodriguez (2007). Starring Rose McGowen, Freddy Rodriguez, Bruce Willis.

A bio-nerve gas is released at a Texan military base, turning the local population into flesh-eating zombies. Stripper Cherry, her machine-gun fake leg and an assortment of townspeople try to stop the 'sickos' taking over the world. Bruce Willis appeared briefly in a cameo role, but his image and name was used prominently in the movie's marketing to increase sales.

DANCE OF THE DEAD

Director Gregg Bishop (2008). Starring Jared Kusnitz, Greyson Chadwick, Chandler Darby.

It's prom night and the dead are rising. Now it's up to the geeks, nerds and misfits who couldn't get dates to save the day. This Indie zombie-comedy went almost straight to DVD, but received positive reviews for its sharp writing and genuine nerd affection: 'Who are you guys?' 'We're the sci-fi club. We're here to rescue you.'

ZOMBIELAND

Director Ruben Fleischer (2009). Starring Woody Harrelson, Jesse Eisenberg, Emma Stone.

Determined to 'enjoy the little things' four zombie-plague survivors take a road trip to an amusement park armed only with an SUV full of guns and a set of die hard rules ('check the back seat', 'do cardio'). With make-up by the Michael Jackson Thriller artist, *Zombieland* redefined the slapstick zombie genre and became the highest grossing zombie movie in history.

ZOMBIES IN POP

The moment when zombies made their most memorable appearance in popular music was in Michael Jackson's *Thriller* video, released in 1983. Directed by John Landis, the groundbreaking video came to be regarded as a milestone in pop video making, signalling a new relationship between music and film. On its release, the 14-minute video was played on MTV twice an hour, satisfying the viewing publics appetite for the living dead set to a phenomenal soundtrack.

A DATE WITH A ZOMBIE

The video narrative for *Thriller* tells of a 1950s teenager who becomes a werewolf at night, when there is a full moon. We then cut to a cinema scene, and realize that a present-day couple are watching a film. On the way home, they pass a cemetery and zombies appear from the graveyard, chasing after them. To the young woman's amazement, her date suddenly becomes a zombie himself, switching back and forth between his human and zombie selves. As he threatens to tear her throat open, the girl wakes up, realizing it was all a dream. Her date offers to take her home. As the film comes to a close, we see his yellow eyes glint, and realize that he is, indeed, a supernatural being. At the end of a dance sequence, the zombies return to the cemetery, grimacing as they go.

Zombies have often featured in pop music, often in a comical or humorous way. Other notable entries into the zombie hall of pop fame are The Zombies, a British rock band featuring keyboard player Rod Argent and vocalist Colin Blunstone. At the height of the pop British invasion of the US, with Beatlemania at its climax, the Zombies had several memorable hits, including *She's Not There* (1964) and *Tell Her No* (1964). However, even though the group named themselves after the living dead, their appearance was anything but gruesome: during their early years, they appeared as five clean-cut young men, often wearing suits, ties and beatle-style hairdos.

ZOMBIE JAMBOREE

In many cases, zombies have been introduced into the pop world through song lyrics. One such example was the multi-talented West Indian star Harry Belafonte, who made his name with an attractive synthesis of pop and calypso.

Echoing his Caribbean roots, and in particular the myth of the voodoo zombie, one of the songs in his repertoire was called *Zombie Jamboree*. Also known as *Jumbie Jamberee* ('jumbie' being the West Indian word for 'ghost') and *Back to Back*, it was written by Conrad Eugene Mauge Jnr, and over time became a calypso standard. As well as Belafonte's version, which he recorded many times from 1962 on, the song was covered by calypso singer Lord Intruder, and folk-pop revivalists The Kingston Trio. Later, reggae star Peter Tosh and singer songwriter Harry Nilsson, also covered this song.

Many songwriters in pop and rock have used the image of the zombie in their lyrics. Such artists include John Fogerty, best known for his work with Creedence Clearwater Revival, whose 1986 solo album was entitled *Eye of the Zombie*. The album was darker in tone than his previous work, and focussed on the perils of the modern world, including terrorism. Songwriter Tom Petty has also referred to zombies in a song called *Zombie Zoo*, telling of a goth-styled girl painted up and waiting in line to go clubbing. The song appeared on his bestselling 1989 album *Full Moon Fever*. Songwriter Rocky Erikson of the

above: Scene still from the music video for Michael Jackson's Thriller, John Landis, 1983.

13th Floor Elevators, a cult sixties' rock group, reprised the theme with *I Walked with a Zombie*, a track from his 1981 album *The Evil One*. The song referenced the 1940s film of the same name, and was notable for including only one line throughout the entire lyric, namely, 'I walked with a zombie', which was repeated over and over again, in a parody of the relentless stupidity of the lumbering undead.

POLITICAL PROTEST: THE ZOMBIE MYTH

Other zombie references have appeared in the music of Fela Kuti, on his album *Zombie*, released in 1977. This time, the reference had a strong political aspect, rather than being simply an entertaining take on the horror genre. Kuti's album was a searing indictment of the behaviour of the Nigerian government and its soldiers, whom he likened to zombies. The government responded to Kuti's criticism with an attack on the commune that he had set up in Nigeria, in which he was beaten, and his elderly mother was killed, sustaining fatal injuries from a fall. Undaunted, Kuti had his mother's coffin delivered to the army barracks in Lagos, as a reminder of what the soldiers had done. Later, in a concert in Accra, riots broke out during a performance of the song *Zombie*.

Once again, the zombie myth was referred to in a protest song by the Irish group The Cranberries, on the 1994 album *No Need to Argue*. The song concerned the troubles in Northern Ireland, and was written by the singer, Dolores O'Riordan. It swapped the light pop sound for which the group was known for a heavier electric mood, with a strong guitar riff. It was extremely successful, and led to a video in which O'Riordan appears covered in gold make-up and standing in front of a cross, with footage of British soldiers on patrol in Northern Ireland cut in. The video was a political comment on the Easter Rising of Irish Republicans against the British in 1916, and criticised Britain's continuing military presence in Northern Ireland.

NIGHT ZOMBIES

'They are Night Zombies!! They are Neighbors!! They Have Come Back from the Dead. Ahhhh!!!' Thus ran the title of one of the songs written by acclaimed American songwriter and musician Sufjan Stevens. It featured on the concept album *Illinoise (Sufjan Stevens invites you to: Come on feel the Illinoise)*, released in 2005, which took as its subject matter the people and places of the US state. Stevens had earlier released an album called *Michigan*, and expressed his intention to release one for each state of the united states; however, he eventually decided to abandon this extended project. *Illinois* was a critically and commercially successful album, containing a variety of intriguing songs, most controversially, one about the infamous serial killer of the region, entitled, 'John Wayne Gacy, Jr'.

As with vampires and werewolves, the zombie today is one of the seminal figures of the horror genre, and zombie lore has become a staple of popular culture, presented not only on the cinema screen, but also as an element of pop and rock music.

ZOMBIE LITERATURE

The roots of zombie fiction can be traced back to the nineteenth century publication of Mary Shelley's *Frankenstein*. While not strictly a zombie novel, it paved the way for later twentieth century writers of the undead such as H.P. Lovecraft and Richard Matheson whose influential works in turn crossed over into the movies. However, it was not until the last decade of the twentieth century that zombie fiction began to emerge as a separate literary genre.

This began with the appearance of *Book of the Dead* and its sequel, *Still Dead: Book of the Dead 2*, published in 1990 and 1992 respectively. Edited by horror writers Craig Spector and John Skipp, the *Book of the Dead* was a collection of modern zombie horror stories, some of them written by famous authors such as Stephen King.

CITY OF THE DEAD

In the new millennium, authors such as Brian Keene have continued this trend with novels such as *The Rising* and *City of the Dead*, telling stories of zombie apocalypse and demonic possession. The master of horror fiction himself, Stephen King, has also mined the zombie literary seam with *Cell*, which was published in 2006 and went on to become a number-one bestseller. The narrative centres on a zombie apocalypse caused by an electromagnetic phenomenon affecting users of mobile phones, who become ravening zombie hordes as a result of their infection.

WORLD WAR Z

In the same year, author Max Brooks published *World War Z*, which also became a bestseller, following the success of his non-fiction *Zombie Survival Guide*, a humorous guide to surviving a zombie attack. This subject is also covered, more seriously, by Jonathan Maberry in his *Zombie CSU: The Forensics of the Living Dead*, in which he discusses how the apparatus of state, from the military to the medical and scientific, would react to a zombie apocalypse.

The zombie theme was also used in David Wellington's trilogy, *Monster Island*, *Monster Nation* and *Monster Planet*, about zombies who lust after a type of golden energy found in living beings. Also contributing to zombie lore is Philip Pullman, with his celebrated fantasy trilogy, *His Dark Materials*. In his books, Pullman describes human beings as having a 'daemon' or soul, which takes shape as an animal companion who constantly accompanies him or her throughout life. Sometimes, a person can be separated from this companion by a process called 'intercision', and as a result, becomes a zombie, with no free will, leading a miserable existence. Similarly, J.K. Rowling of the Harry Potter series, tells of Inferi, dead human beings who can be reanimated by black magic.

ZOMBIE MASH-UP

The most recent literary zombie phenomenon has been the 'zombie mash-up novel' which combines a classic text with a narrative about a zombie outbreak, and has been literary sensation. *Pride and Prejudice and Zombies* by Seth Grahame-Smith interleaves Jane Austen's classic text with a story about zombies, giving the entire novel a new slant. One critic wrote of it, 'What begins as a gimmick ends with renewed appreciation of the indomitable appeal of Austen's language, characters, and situations.' Also published in 2009 was *Sense and Sensibility and Sea Monsters*, which gave another of Austen's novels the same treatment.

QC

QUIRK
CLASSICS

PRIDE AND PREJUDICE
AND ZOMBIES

BY JANE AUSTEN AND S... ...AME-SMITH

TOP ZOMBIE BOOKS

FRANKENSTEIN

Mary Shelley. Published 1818. One of the most remarkable science fiction stories ever written. Not so much a zombie story more a novel of fear, horror and despair. Amazingly, Mary Shelley was only 19 when she wrote it. The monster is very different from the iconic Boris Karloff squarehead and bolts monster of the classic 1931 Hollywood horror movie. He is an agile, resourceful and calculating creature who can clearly articulate his thoughts, while the dark side of his character is carrying out horrible, shocking murders. A lot is left to the imagination. He has no name. We never find out how Frankenstein creates the monster nor indeed what the monster really looks like. Written in 1818, it is undoubtedly a masterpiece and essential, classic reading.

THE ZOMBIE SURVIVAL GUIDE

Max Brooks. Duckworth (2004). This book explains all you need to completely protect yourself from flesh-eating living dead. Brooks reinvents zombie history, naming Solanum as the virus that causes the 'undead plague'. It attacks the brain and allows it to keep functioning even after the body begins to decompose. Feeling no pain, and having no awareness of the world around them except for the food on offer, Brooks' zombies are a modern evolution of the Romero zombie in the 1968 cult classic, *Night of the Living Dead*. Readers have been know to rush out and buy an axe for protection after studying the recommendation that shotguns and chainsaws look great in videos but are no good in a post apocalypse scenario when you are out of shells and out of gas! A short spin-off *The Zombie Survival Guide: Recorded Attacks* was published in 2009.

WORLD WAR Z

Max Brooks. Duckworth(2007). Written as a retrospective history of a zombie war where the human race is almost wiped out by a global zombie pandemic. The story is told from the point of view of a UN-appointed interviewer, who has travelled the world to get first-hand accounts from those survivors who played significant roles in humanity's desperate fight-back and eventual victory against the zombies. The gripping much-praised sequel to *The Zombie Survival Guide*.

ZOMBIE HAIKU: GOOD POETRY FOR YOUR BRAINS

Ryan Mecum. How Design Books (2008).
An original spin on the zombie story and perfect for zombiephiles, video game addicts and horror movie fanatics. *Zombie Haiku* is the touching story of a zombie's gradual decay told through the intimate poetry of haiku. From infection to demise, readers accompany the narrator on a journey through deserted streets and barracaded doors for every eye-popping, gut-wrenching, flesh-eating moment

T. Holst, del.   W. Chevalier, sculp.

FRANKENSTEIN.

right up to the inevitable bullet to the brain. The haikus form an actual story, instead of just being random haikus. They're all three lines long - the first and third have five syllables and the second line has seven syllables. They're all written from the point of view of a zombie as he searches for brains to eat. Ingenious and very entertaining.

THE LIVING DEAD

Various authors. Night Shade Books (2008).
This is not a normal collection of zombie fiction. *The Living Dead* has contributions from some of the most talented horror writers of modern times and every one of them is very readable. If you are a fan of zombies, horror or simply good writing then this anthology is for you. However, beware, even though it is all about zombies, hardly any of the stories feature the usual survivors gunning down hordes of the shambling head-exploding undead.

PRIDE AND PREJUDICE AND ZOMBIES

Jane Austen and Seth Graeme-Smith. Quirk Books (2009).
Fun and entertaining. The first classic 'mash-up', but 90% Pride and Prejudice and 10% Zombies. The zombies are very much a background story, and only very occasionally do they pop up in the story line. Zombies have been plaguing the English countryside for years. It's no longer safe to venture out alone. The Bennet family are experts at dealing with the undead and are all martial arts warriors The book mixes the

new and old and rewrites Jane Austen sentences to fit the plot. An original concept with an eye-catching cover and illustrations.

ZOMPOC: HOW TO SURVIVE A ZOMBIE APOCALYPSE

Michael and Nick Thomas. Swordworks (2009).
Lurching along in the footsteps of Max Brooks comes a survival manual to keep you safe during the Zompoc (Zombie Apocalypse). All zombie strains from the viral infected fast zombies through to the shambling re-animated undead are identified. It teaches you how to fight different types of zombies, choose suitable weaponry and armour vehicles, Useful tips to defend your home and family and form a survival group. Keep this handy family reference manual close by for the fast-approaching, inevitable day of the Zompoc.

ZOMBIES FOR ZOMBIES: ADVICE AND ETIQUETTE FOR THE UNDEAD

David P. Murphy. Sourcebooks (2009).
The first motivational guide for the undead. This guide shows zombies how to preserve their quality of life. Contains brain recipes, and dance steps designed to accommodate the zombies' total lack of flexibility. There is a very instructive chapter on zombie sex entitled 'The Coma Sutra'. Fun for those interested in adopting the zombie life style.

ZOMBIE COMICS

Tales from the Crypt was the first comic anthology to feature zombie-like characters back in the 1950s as discussed earlier (see page 110). Zombies didn't appear in comics again until the mid 1970s after George Romero had given the living dead a resurgence with his zombie films.

TALES OF THE ZOMBIE

Marvel Comics (1973-75). The Zombie (Simon William Garth) is a supernatural character who starred in the black-and-white, horror-comic series *Tales of the Zombie* in stories mostly by Steve Gerber and artist Pablo Marcos. The character first appeared 20 years earlier in the standalone story *Zombie* by Stan Lee and Bill Everett published in the horror comic *Menace # 5* in July 1953 by Atlas Comics.

As the Zombie, Garth has super human strength yet is also able to gently heal other people's injuries magically. Alas he is also totally mindless and must obey anyone who has a duplicate of the Amulet of Damballah, which he wears around his neck. Despite his zombie state, he retains some human traits, on occasion showing the ability to act of his own freewill when friends or people he loved when alive come under threat. Voodoo is his biggest weakness, (he met his death as a voodoo cult's human sacrifice). Garth is continually being put under voodoo spells and forced to carry out evil acts under the orders of arch enemy protagonists of the story lines, such as the voodoo witch Calypso. However Garth's freewill usually asserts itself in the nick of time and he saves the day by ignoring the evil orders. Finally laid to rest in *Tales of the Zombie # 9*, Garth has been occasionally reanimated for guest appearances in Spiderman and in some solo stories. He is also one of the main characters in *Marvel Zombies #4*.

THE WALKING DEAD

Image Comics (2003). This long-running black and white American monthly comic book was created by writer Robert Kirkman and artist Tony Moore (replaced by Charlie Adlard from issue #7 onward). It chronicles the travels of a group of people trying to survive in a world stricken by a zombie apocalypse Starring Rick Grimes, a small-town police officer from Cynthiana, Kentucky, his family, and a number of other survivors who have banded together in order to survive after the world is overrun with zombies. As the series progresses, the characters become more developed, and their personalities shift under the stress of a never-ending zombie apocalypse. In 2010, the comic book is being made into a US television series, which the creators hope will be just as long running.

MARVEL ZOMBIES

Marvel Comics (2005-06).
A five-issue limited series written by Robert Kirkman with art by Sean Phillips and covers by Arthur Suydam. The story is that almost all super-powered beings on Earth including the Fantastic Four become flesh-eating zombies after being infected by an alien virus. The

infection spreads via contact with the blood of the victim, usually through a bite by an infected individual. The zombified superbeings largely retain their intellect and personality, although they are constantly driven by the hunger for fresh meat. *The Marvel Zombies* concept first appeared in Ultimate Fantastic Four #21-23 (2005)

In a sequel to the original series, the five-issue *Marvel Zombies 2*, was published from October 2007 to February 2008, and *Marvel Zombies 3* a four-issue series, commenced October 2008. *Marvel Zombies 4* is a four-issue limited series published over the summer of 2009 featuring characters from Marvel's horror comics (Man-Thing, The Zombie, Morbius the Living Vampire, Werewolf by Night, and Mephisto among others). *Marvel Zombies Return* is a five-issue series started in September 2009, and is a sequel to *Marvel Zombies 2*.

THE ZOMBIE HUNTERS (TZH)

Canadian webcomic (2006).
Written and illustrated by Jenny Romanchuk, the characters are based on friends in her hometown of Sault Ste Marie in Ontario, Canada. The comic all started as a joke for her friends but has become a long term ongoing web project.

The story is about a group who live in a small island colony of human survivors preserving civilisation after a zombie virus outbreak. The twist in this particular zombie story is that the zombie virus causes zombification in humans only after death. Most of the population of the island is infected by the dormant virus.

ZOMBIE COMPUTER GAMES

Although it defined a new genre in computer gaming, over the years, *Zombie Zombie*, the very first video game about zombies, released for the ZX Spectrum in 1984, has nearly been forgotten. Inspired by the movies of George Romero, the aim of *Zombie Zombie* was to terminate the city's zombie infestation by killing as many zombs as possible. The game has long been lost in obscurity. However, it was an historic first step, creating the zombie survival-horror genre that remains one of gaming's most popular themes today.

GHOST 'N GOBLINS

Capcom (1985).
This classic platform arcade game was one of the first to introduce the undead into gaming. The player helps Sir Arthur rescue his princess by slaughtering hordes of brightly-coloured zombies, which rise from the ground to attack him. Regarded as one of the most difficult games ever released and Sir Arthur can only be hit twice before dying and has a time limit to complete each level. Good luck!

ALONE IN THE DARK

Infogames (1992).
The series that started the popular 3D survival-horror genre stars private investigator Edward Carnby, who is sent to investigate a haunted mansion/town/park, crawling with the undead. Gameplay integrates puzzle solving with zombie-massacring, and allows the gamer to pick up any object and use it as a weapon. Alone was one of the first two games to use polygonal characters over pre-rendered backgrounds.

ZOMBIES ATE MY NEIGHBORS

LucasArts (1993).
This platform game features Zeke and Julie who save helpless victims and battle monsters with an assortment of weapons, including silverware, dishes, keys and bazookas. The game pays homage to every B-grade horror movie ever made, with its lumbering 1950s monsters and a kooky soundtrack. Censors in Europe ordered revisions before its release, including shortening the name to 'Zombies' and replacing the chainsaw-wielding maniacs with lumberjacks carrying axes. As with all LucasArts products it is a big-time game worthy of any collection.

RESIDENT EVIL

Capcom (1996).

The big-daddy of zombie computer games and the first game to be termed 'a survival-horror' *Resident Evil* sold millions of copies, spawned five sequels (the sixth is coming) and three movie spin offs. Generally considered to have redefined the genre forever. Gameplay in this third-person action adventure means survival in a creepy mansion, inhabited by you-know-what. Taking on the role of a Special Tactics and Rescue Service officer the player must uncover the mystery of the mansion and escape alive. Some of the *Resident Evils* do follow the *28 Days* lead with viruses turning people into running zombies rather

than pure zombies lurching undead from the grave. *Resident Evil 2* is considered by game players to be the best of the sequels, although it arouses much controversy trying to pick a favourite from the series!

HOUSE OF THE DEAD SERIES

Sega (1996).

House of the Dead I, II, III, & IV is one of the most popular shooter classics. A zombie death shootfest developed by Sega as a light-gun video arcade game in 1996 and later ported to the Dreamcast, PC and X-box. The game is now also available for Wii with a hand cannon providing an authentic arcade feel. A horror-survival classic based around mowing down waves of infected, blood-thirsty zombs in a last-ditch effort to survive and get out of town.

House of the Dead Overkill, a prequel to the other games in the series, takes the zombie shooter in a new direction, injecting a retro B-movie look. But the blood-splattering, head-exploding action is unchanged.

SILENT HILL

Konami (1999).
The first in a series of three, this survival-horror game focuses on Harry Mason, who is searching for his daughter in Silent Hill, an off-season resort town, which is about to be overtaken by a hellish otherworld. With its eerie piping music, and creepy Japanese horror film atmosphere, *Silent Hill* has been called the scariest game ever made and needed several design revisions before being released into the European market. Maybe not strictly zombies, more like weird evil monsters from another dimension, but very scary. Especially when played in the dark in the middle of the night ... aaaaagh!

THEY HUNGER

Black Widow Games (1999)
Released as a series of three, this first-person shooter takes the

role of a writer who has escaped to the country to compose his next novel. But on the way his car crashes and he ends up in an underground catacomb. Zombies ensue. Technically, *They Hunger* is a modification of another game, *Half-Life*. *Half-Life* is the biggest, most owned, most played, best-loved and gigantic series of games ever. *They Hunger* features the same revolver, types of ammunition and sound clips as the original.

STUBBS THE ZOMBIE IN REBEL WITHOUT A PULSE

Wideload Games (2005).
This third-person action-game turns the horror genre on is head by making the player the zombie. Stubbs lurches through the futuristic city of Punchbowl battling mad scientists, rural militiamen and a lethal barbershop quartet. US Senator Joe Lieberman criticised the game as 'cannibalistic', and harmful to underage children. The designers retorted, that: 'Stubbs is a zombie. Thus the title "Stubbs the Zombie". Zombies eat brains. That's what they do.'

DEAD RISING

Capacom (2006).
This action-adventure-survival-horror centres on a photojournalist trapped in a shopping mall infested with zombies, crazed psychopaths and survivors. The player can use 250 different objects as weapons and has to complete missions to gain points. The MKR Group, which holds the copyright to the Romero film *Dawn of the Dead*, tried to sue Capacom for using the zombie outbreak in a mall idea, but the case was dismissed. A new sequel *Dead Rising 2* is now available. Considered to be even better than the original.

LEFT 4 DEAD

Turtle Rock Studios (2008).
A great award winning game. This cooperative first-person shooter is set in the aftermath of an apocalyptic pandemic and pits four protagonists against hordes of zombies. There are four different game modes: single player, four-player cooperative, eight-player online, and four-player survival. Ex-Faith No More singer Mike Patton helped create the voices of the infected, drawing inspiration from *Dawn of the Dead* and *28 Days Later*. A new improved sequel *Left 4 Dead 2* has recently been released with a fanfare of web, TV and cinema trailers. It looks set to become the new King of Zombies in the ever changing world of computer games

KILLING FLOOR

Tripwire Interactive (2009).
Gameplay in this cooperative first-person shooter consists of slaughtering wave after wave of zombies, or 'humanoid specimens', who are out on the prowl for human flesh. The grand finale is a showdown with the 'patriarch', the chain-gun wielding king zombie, who has powers of invisibility. *Killing Floor* was a top seller in 2009 and received mainly positive reviews, but was also criticised for being too repetitive.

INDEX

This edition published in 2010 by
CHARTWELL BOOKS, INC.
A division of BOOK SALES, INC.
276 Fifth Avenue Suite 206
New York, New York 10001
USA

© 2010 Omnipress Limited
www.omnipress.co.uk

Reprinted 2011, 2012

ISBN-13: 978-0-7858-2654-5
ISBN-10: 0-7858-2654-8

Canary Press
An imprint of Omnipress Ltd
Chantry House, 22 Upperton Road
Eastbourne, East Sussex BN21 1BF
England

Printed in China